SMOLDER

FLASHPOINT BOOK 2

TARA ELLIS

MIKE KRAUS

Tara Ellis
♡
2019

MUONIC
PRESS

SMOLDER
The Flashpoint Series
Book 2

By
Tara Ellis
Mike Kraus

© 2019 Muonic Press Inc
www.muonic.com

* * *

www.facebook.com/taraellisauthor

* * *

www.MikeKrausBooks.com
hello@mikeKrausBooks.com
www.facebook.com/MikeKrausBooks

CONTENTS

WANT MORE AWESOME BOOKS?

Find more fantastic tales at books.to/readmorepa.

If you're new to reading Mike Kraus, consider visiting his website at MikeKrausBooks.com and signing up for his free newsletter. You'll receive several free books and a sample of his audiobooks, too, just for signing up, you can unsubscribe at any time and you will receive absolutely *no* spam.

* * *

You can also stay updated on Tara's books by following her Facebook page: www.facebook.com/taraellisauthor

SPECIAL THANKS

Special thanks to my awesome beta team, without whom this book wouldn't be nearly as great.

Thank you!

PROLOGUE

The Earth has been impacted by a gamma-ray burst, the most powerful explosion in the known universe. With half the population killed instantly and the other half dying, those struggling to survive are slowly coming to realize the lasting consequences.

Stranded hundreds of miles from home, we follow the converging stories of a group of survivors connected by a town called Mercy. Each of them is drawn to the small town for different reasons, but all of them want to survive.

Danny was already questioning her role in life when the event occurred, but facing death has a way of clarifying what's important. As she and her new friend Sam travel five hundred miles to where her father lives in Mercy, Montana, the paramedic may discover more about herself than she ever wanted to know.

Tom and his son Ethan started their trek over a hundred miles north of Danny, but they have the same destination. The cattle ranch has been in Tom's family for multiple generations and is the perfect refuge in the unfolding apocalypse...if they can get there.

Back in Mercy, Mayor Patty does her best to pull the town together in the face of the world-altering event, yet even the small-town community mentality might not be enough. Fear and desperation spread quickly and the leaders of Mercy must come together and rally against it.

In the steep terrain surrounding the mountain town, a group of troubled teens are led by well-meaning counselors on a survivalist hike when they find themselves cut off and without any means of retreat. Running low on supplies, they set out across the national forest to find their only hope of sanctuary, the people of Mercy.

While most of the threats the survivors face are tangible, another, more insidious evil looms on the horizon. Someone else is coming to Mercy.

CHAPTER 1

Dallas Medical Center, Dallas, Texas

DR. ELIZABETH GREY pulled the soiled sheet up, covering the face of her patient. Jack had also been a friend, co-worker, and occasional lover. She should have felt more. The chill that had settled into her stomach and then spread through her body over the past five days as the body count rose had stolen that from her. Now, there was a hollowness that only widened and threatened to swallow her as she stood there, staring down at the unmoving sheet.

"Lizzy."

Elizabeth jumped and spun around to face the dark hall behind her, fighting the wave of severe nausea caused by the movement. The voice was broken and dry, like that of someone who'd been stranded out in the dessert for days. Only her friends called her Lizzy and she'd thought they were all dead. She took the green glowstick from Jack's bedside. He wouldn't be needing it anymore.

Five days. Five days since the flash had plunged them all into a living nightmare. The faint light from the glowstick didn't do much more than cast a green hue a few feet around her, revealing a stark hospital hallway that had been transformed into something that was barely recognizable. Pausing, she bent over and retched onto the floor, ignoring the bloody streaks mixed in with the bile.

Elizabeth wiped at her mouth with the back of her hand and then stood for a moment, listening. Someone was moaning at the other end of the hall, and a woman was wailing in the distance. Probably from the ER. Any patients who arrived in the past two days were all outside. Those still inside had either recovered enough to leave or had died. Family members wandered around aimlessly with candles, desperately looking for loved ones.

But she'd recognized the voice that whispered her name.

Elizabeth had been an ER physician at the large, urban medical center for over a decade and she knew most of the staff. They were her family. Choking back an unexpected sob, Elizabeth stepped over a body and held the glowstick out at arm's length. "Hello?" Her voice sounded foreign to her. She knew she was dehydrated, her body ravaged by radiation, and it was only a matter of time before she joined the silenced forms blanketing the floors.

"Lizzy...are you there?"

Elizabeth jabbed the inadequate light to her left, revealing an open door. She didn't have to see much to know where she was. She could walk the length of the administrative wing of the hospital with her eyes closed. "Pam!"

Pam Elliott was the Chief Nursing Director and her best friend. Pam disappeared two days earlier, after her daughter died in her arms in the parking lot. Now, Elizabeth could see she was sitting cross-legged on the floor, in the dark, holding a bag of IV fluids. She'd bitten the top off and was drinking it.

"What are you doing?" Elizabeth dropped to her knees and grabbed at the bag. Pam pulled back, cuddling the solution to her chest. Her eyes were wild, her lips parched, and she had clearly gone over the edge. "Okay," Elizabeth placated, falling back onto her bottom and putting her hands out in surrender. "Drink it if you can stomach it. I guess it really doesn't matter." She eyed the bag, as surprised to see it as she was her friend. They'd run out of them less than twenty-four hours after it all began.

The hospital was immediately overrun after the flash, with patients ranging from car accident victims to severe sunburns, as well as injuries from the fires raging in the city. Those were the ones that could make it to the hospital on foot or be carried. Since they were in the center of a sprawling metropolis with a population of nearly one-and-a-half-million, it was a feat easily accomplished for far too many.

The radiation poisoning symptoms began by nightfall on the first day. By then, Elizabeth had already blown through most of the supplies in the ER. They'd moved their triage out into the parking lot, both for space and natural light, and even that over-flowed in a matter of hours.

She didn't know a lot about radiation, but it didn't take a genius to make the connection between the event and the obvious symptoms. Whatever had caused the light, it had also unleashed some sort of radiation that had devastating effects. Most of her staff abandoned their posts the first day; Elizabeth understood why. They had families, children they had to try and get home to. Those who remained, like herself and Jack, she'd quickly dosed with IV fluids and anti-nausea meds so that they could keep treating their patients.

If they'd had enough staff, supplies, and power, Elizabeth believed that most of the people who'd been healthy before falling ill could have recovered. As it was, by the third day, there wasn't anything she could do for them, other than hold their hands while they died.

They were out of water, IV supplies, any useful medications, and vomit bags. The bags were important because their disappearance marked a clear turning point. Without working bathrooms, when the bags were gone, they were out of options. Hundreds of people had defecated bloody diarrhea on the ground, as well as vomiting, threatening to spread disease on top of the radiation sickness. It was unbearable.

Elizabeth wouldn't have come back inside the building if it weren't for Jack. He didn't want to die in an anonymous pile of indistinguishable bodies in the parking lot, so on trembling legs the two of them had made the short pilgrimage to the employee sleep room. They'd shared some fond memories there in previous years.

Elizabeth hung her head and stared for a moment at the green haze in her lap as the disorganized memories tumbled through her mind, confusing her. The light was getting dimmer but it still reminded her of one of her favorite science fiction movies. She blinked slowly, unable to focus enough to remember the name of it.

An explosion from outside rocked the building, briefly illuminating the one window of the office in the predawn darkness. Elizabeth grunted as she staggered to her feet in the roaring aftermath and went to the window. They were on the fourth floor, so she could see the burning city spreading out for miles in every direction. It was a cityscape seared into her memory long ago, now distorted by all of the destruction.

One of the large propane storage tanks located behind the building had exploded and flames were roaring thirty feet into the air above it. She turned away from the imagery on the ground that the light exposed.

"Lizzy, I'll get to see Sarah soon."

Elizabeth jumped at Pam's voice. She'd forgotten her friend was there. Rubbing at her burning eyes, she was briefly tempted to ask for a sip of the IV fluids, even though she knew the saline would only make her situation worse in the end. Instead, she closed the office door, hoping to block out some of the stench during their final hours.

Elizabeth sat down next to Pam, dropped the glowstick on the floor in front of them, and set a hand on her friend's knee. "Yes, Pam. You can see Sarah again."

When Pam slumped over and put her head in Elizabeth's lap, she gently stroked the other woman's hair. "You're a good mom." Elizabeth had never had children of her own, and she regretted it.

Looking up at the window still outlined by the fire, she wondered how long it would be before the sun came up. Maybe she'd start walking. Just...get on the freeway and walk until she couldn't anymore. At least she'd be free of the darkness and stench of the hospital.

Pam took a shuddering breath under her hand and became still.

Elizabeth closed her eyes and pictured the arboretum located several miles away. It was one of her favorite places in the city. She might be able to make it there. Her mother had always liked the flowers and they would spend hours guessing the names.

An overwhelming weariness spread through her and she slid down to the floor, cradling her friend's lifeless body. The dark chasm she'd been narrowly walking broke open and Elizabeth fell into the void with a sort of relief, the pent-up grief escaping as tears finally spilled. "You go see Sarah," she whispered.

CHAPTER 2

Near Honeyville, Utah

A BLINDING white light was all Danny could see. It filled her with dread as it washed out her world then rapidly faded, leaving her blinking in its wake. She was back on the plane, but something was different. Turning to look out the window, instead of planes falling from the sky, it was bodies. Danny recoiled from the scene, unfortunately not before she saw her father land on the wing of the plane with a sickening thud.

Her breath coming in ragged gasps, Danny flailed as hands grabbed at her, pushing her down and covering her mouth. Trying to scream around the fingers, she jerked awake and almost bit the flesh between her teeth before recognizing the face hovering over her.

"We have to go!" Sam growled, his voice urgent.

Danny shook off the remnants of the recurring dream she'd been having every night and tried to focus on their present situation. "Why? What's happening?" She could hear them then, at least two people moving around above them on the old rotten floorboards of the ancient barn they'd taken refuge beneath.

"Call it a cleansing," Sam said cryptically. He already had his pack on and held Danny's out to her. "It's almost morning. Are you up to riding your bike?"

Grabbing the backpack, Danny stood with some effort before struggling into it. Although she was careful, the strap still scraped against the bandage on her left arm, causing her to wince. "Do I have a choice?"

The past thirty-six hours were still pretty fuzzy, but Sam had filled in most of the blanks the last time she'd been awake, earlier that day. "Is it the other guy from the pharmacy?"

Sam grunted. "I wish. It's a lot worse than the brother of the guy I...shot."

Danny understood why Sam couldn't bring himself to say that he'd killed him. She remembered hearing the gunshots while lying on the floor of the backroom of the pharmacy. Then Grace was barking, there were screams, and then another shot. The way Sam described it, the golden retriever attacked the man who'd shot at him. Sam had then picked up the dropped weapon, just in time to see another guy aiming at him. Sam didn't have a choice. It was either kill or be killed.

Following Sam across the cramped space of the storm cellar, Danny's headache made her already short patience non-existent. She glanced up as another board creaked. "*Who* is it then, Sam?"

"When I went back to the park for your bike, the purge was already underway." Sam paused at the sound of a slamming door from the structure above them, and lowered his voice. "I guess the sheriff's plan to keep things orderly involves closing the town off and getting rid of any outsiders. From what I saw, it's by any means necessary."

Unfortunately, their plan to enter the smaller town had backfired. For the same reasons she and Sam thought it would be safe, the fact that the community wasn't totally disbanded now worked against them.

The irony was that they *had* stolen from the town's pharmacy, and in the process, someone was killed. It didn't matter who was at fault. Danny rubbed at her healing arm. Was it worth it?

The park where they'd originally stored their things, near the small town of Honeyville, had become a sort of refugee camp. With the temperature around a hundred for several days and no running water or power for air conditioning, some residents were also turning to the park and had started to clash with the drifters.

Danny wasn't surprised things were coming to a head, it just would have been nice if they'd gotten out of town first. She reached to extinguish the small candle burning on the dirt floor. She still wasn't sure how Sam managed to get her down there in her weakened state. Rather than trying to go back through the main part of town, he'd opted to get her as far north as he could. It turned out to be a great refuge, without any windows to reveal their light and a stream close by with fresh water.

"Why are they looking for us here?" she asked, frustrated

Sam cautiously pushed the cellar door open while Danny crept up the steps behind him. Grace whined as the sounds above them intensified and Danny stopped to rest a hand on the dog's shoulders to quiet her. The last thing they needed was for her to bark.

Sam surveyed the field before waving for Danny to follow him. Thankfully, the storm cellar was behind the barn and the men looking for them probably didn't even know it was there. "Someone must have seen me earlier when I got your bike."

Danny fought against a wave of dizziness as she scurried after Sam. They made their way through the field and into a cluster of nearby trees. She leaned against the trunk of a pine and took a breath to settle her stomach.

"You good?" Sam asked. He sounded skeptical and was eyeing her closely while uncovering their bikes.

"Good as new." She'd been on the antibiotics for almost thirty-six hours and her fever had been gone for twelve. If her nose was a good judge, the meds were knocking out the infection in her arm. She'd be okay, and in a couple of more days she'd have her strength back. Dehydration from the high fever and vomiting was her concern now. Without the option of IV fluids, she had to conquer it the old-fashioned way. She rummaged for her water bottle at the thought and gulped as much as she could stomach.

A flicker of light caught Danny's attention as she wiped at her mouth and she looked to the south with growing astonishment. "Is the park on fire?"

"They were starting to burn the tents when I left," Sam replied. "It...was an ugly scene."

Danny watched as the growing flames licked at the tops of the trees lining the creek. They'd gone insane. If it crossed the water, the rest of the town could burn as well.

"How long do you think it'll be before we see some sign of the military?" Danny asked as she lifted her bike. The growing chaos was a poignant reminder of the government's lack of response. She strained to see Sam's expression in the early pre-dawn light. She'd come to know the older man fairly well over the past five days and she could tell something else was up. "Sam?"

Sam silently straddled his bike and looked over at her. "There might not be much of a government left. I'm not sure who'd be giving the orders, how they'd give them, or how what's left of the military would organize and deploy."

They remained hidden in the trees, waiting for the men searching the barn to leave. Danny rubbed absently at her arm, wishing she'd taken some more Advil earlier. "Wouldn't the military have equipment that was shielded from the EMP?"

"Probably," Sam agreed. "Although, this wasn't a normal EMP, and if there isn't anyone alive to operate what *does* work, then it doesn't matter." He dropped the bike and attempted to walk past her.

Danny stopped him with a hand on his arm. "Talk to me," she said to Sam's back.

Shoulders sagging, Sam took an audible breath before turning to face her. "There's a rumor going around…from more than one source, according to the person I talked to tonight, that everyone on the East Coast is—dead."

Danny recoiled. "Dead? How could everyone be dead?"

"Radiation." Sam reached out to pet Grace, unable to meet Danny's eyes. "They're calling it the flashpoint, the point of impact of the gamma-ray. We were right about where it struck. It was far to the southeast, beyond our continent. But we're over two thousand miles west of the coast, Danny, and apparently that distance makes a big difference in the amount of gamma radiation exposure. We might have mild illness, but the eastern half of the country wasn't as lucky."

Danny refused to believe that millions were already dead. "How can anyone be sure?"

"Radios." Sam jammed his hands into his jeans' pockets. "Ham radios. I guess it's common practice for enthusiasts to shield their radios. It's easy to do and they can communicate over long distances."

Danny struggled to absorb the information. *Everyone on the East Coast was dead.* Gasping, she dropped her bike and stepped in front of Sam. "Your wife!" She knew they'd been visiting his in-laws on the Florida coast and he'd left early to return for a chemistry convention. His wife was still there. "I'm so sorry."

"It doesn't change anything," Sam said gruffly. "She'd want me to survive. So…let's survive."

The door of the barn slammed open and Danny could see two people walk outside. After a few tense minutes they headed in the opposite direction, back toward town. Relieved, she glanced over at Sam and her smile faded when she saw that he was holding the gun he'd gotten at the pharmacy. "Would you have shot them?"

Sam stared down at the gun, turning it over in his hands before sliding it into his back pocket. "Like I said, Danny. Let's survive."

Once they were safely peddling up the dirt road that would lead them back to the interstate, Danny looked over at Sam. The sun hadn't crested the horizon yet, but the intense northern lights were still bright enough that she could at least see his silhouette. "Thank you for taking care of me."

Sam chuckled. "I figure you'll probably get the chance to repay me at some point."

Danny smiled at her friend, although she doubted he could see it. Another wave of dizziness forced her to concentrate on the road in front of her. She'd been taking Zofran, a strong anti-nausea medication, but it made her light-headed. Guilt tugged at her as she thought of the hoard they had stashed in the bottom of her pack.

They'd been lucky to find several useful things in the pharmacy, although there wasn't very much of it. As a paramedic, it went against her nature to withhold it from other people who needed it just as much as she did. Nevertheless, Sam was right. They were in a fight for their lives and whether it be passive or aggressive, she was already in survival mode.

For whatever reason, not everyone was as sensitive to the radiation as others. Danny suspected it had to do with the immune system and underlying illnesses or conditions. She figured that, given where they were when the gamma radiation had hit, it was mild enough that so long as they could keep some water down while their bodies repaired whatever damage was caused by it, they'd be okay.

Sam's symptoms hadn't progressed beyond a mild headache and some nausea. Grace had thrown up twice but appeared to be doing better, despite a bout of whining and whimpering. Danny didn't dare push things by turning and looking behind them; she knew the golden retriever was back there, plodding along after them. She had amazing stamina.

"We should make it into Idaho by tonight," Sam offered.

Danny smiled. Idaho. Although it was an imaginary line, it still meant they were getting closer to home. Closer to Mercy.

CHAPTER 3

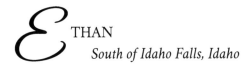THAN
South of Idaho Falls, Idaho

"THEY'RE FREAKING *GARDENING* SHEARS, man. It isn't going to work!"

Ethan cringed as spittle flew from Billy's mouth and spattered on his forehead. He resisted the urge to wipe at it and instead concentrated on the task at hand. It had somehow become *his* responsibility to free Decker and Billy from their shackles. Well, pretty much everything was his job. Including caring for the horses, starting a fire, tending the fire, cooking all the meals, cleaning up, packing...and stealing whatever the convicts told him to.

They were kneeling in brown, brittle grass surrounding an old barn. It was early morning and the sun was just starting to paint the tips of the trees at the edge of the sprawling farm. They'd come upon it in the middle of the night and stopped next to a pond to sleep. As soon as Decker woke and saw the tool shed, he'd sent Ethan looking for something that might break the chains.

Ethan gave in and wiped at his forehead when a bead of sweat mixed in with the spit, and was rewarded with a slap to his ear from Decker. The bigger of the two men was also the smarter and meaner one. He enjoyed intimidating both Ethan and Billy, and Ethan's ear was raw and bleeding from the number of hits it'd taken over the past two nights. But Ethan knew it could be worse. It could be a lot worse. He tried not to think of his dad, lying there in the road, shot and unconscious. Was he even still alive?

"Hey!"

Ethan ducked in anticipation which elicited an unsettling laugh from Decker. He hated the man.

"Concentrate, shrimp. Unless you want to wake our hosts up." Decker drew the Glock he'd taken off the dead guard from the bus and waved it towards the small farmhouse before putting it away again.

Ethan swallowed. He'd been doing his best to keep the two convicts from interacting with anyone else. So far, he'd been lucky. The stretch of freeway they were backtracking was still relatively barren and most of the people they passed were happy to keep to themselves.

They were headed for Pocatello. Ethan had warned Decker that the city was literally on fire, but the man was adamant. His destination was actually a place south of the bigger town, but they still had to go either through it or around it.

The first thing Ethan learned after being taken was that Decker had a poor sense of direction. He didn't believe Ethan at first when he told the escaped convict that he'd been heading the wrong way ever since he walked away from the bus crash. It wasn't until Ethan dug the map out and showed him that Decker grudgingly turned south, threatening to permanently silence Billy if he said anything about it.

Ethan made sure to trot Tango in loose soil whenever he had a chance. He knew his dad would track them and since they were on a freeway, horse prints along the side of the road weren't that hard to spot. He also said hello and smiled at anyone they passed, hoping they might remember him. If his dad was alive, he'd be coming for him.

There hadn't been much in the way of options the past day, as far as looking for tools. They'd ridden past Idaho Falls in the dark the first night and since then, things had been sparse. As they got closer to some other, smaller towns, the fields were becoming dotted with more houses and Ethan had known the time was coming when the men would get more insistent on being freed. He stayed awake the first night, waiting for an opportunity to run, though it never presented itself. Last night he'd been too tired and fell asleep. Now, if he somehow managed to get their cuffs off, he'd probably never get away from them on his own.

"You try, Decker!" Billy urged. "The kid isn't strong enough."

Decker grunted and shoved Ethan aside, knocking him onto his back. A rooster crowed and he looked nervously at the farmhouse. He wasn't sure what the men would do if they were confronted by someone. He'd tried at first to stay in the barn, but it was too dark in there to see what they were doing. Although, that also had its advantages.

"Ugh!" Decker grumbled. He threw the shears, now in two pieces, onto the ground.

"You broke 'em!" Billy wailed. "Man, it didn't hardly even dent the chain."

"Shut up!" Decker yelled. He strode over to a wood pile up against the barn and pulled an axe from a stump. A ray of sunlight glinted off the sharpened blade as he made his way back with it. "You want 'em off?" He lifted the axe. "Then stick your hands out, Billy! Come on!"

Billy scooted backwards in the dirt; his eyes wild with fear. "You're crazy! Get away from me with that. You'll miss and cut my hand off!"

"Then I won't have to listen to you moan and complain about it anymore!" Decker swung the axe, and Ethan thought he might actually do it, but it struck the ground at the other man's feet.

"What's going on out here?"

Ethan's stomach went cold when he saw a middle-aged man coming down off the porch of the house, a rifle in his hand, although it wasn't raised. He jumped to his feet and tried to intervene. "It's okay! We're just leaving. Our...horses needed water."

The man hesitated and looked from Ethan to the other two rugged men. They'd changed out of their prison garb and into his dad's spare clothes they'd taken, but their cuffed hands were clearly on display. He started to raise the rifle. "I'm afraid I'm going to have to ask you to be on your way."

Decker took two long steps in the homeowner's direction, pushing Ethan out of the way and knocking him down again. As he did so, Ethan saw the Glock in his hand. "You wouldn't happen to have a blowtorch hidden around here somewhere, would you?"

"A blowtorch?" The man looked pointedly at the cuffs on Decker's wrists, and the gun clutched in his hand, and made a motion to pull the bolt action on the old .22.

"I didn't think so." Decker took another quick step to narrow the distance and then shot twice, dropping the man before he'd completed the action. His body fell silently, an almost gentle gesture that added to Ethan's confusion. How could a man's life be taken with such little fanfare?

"No!" A woman had appeared in the doorway, a small boy at her side. "What have you done?"

Decker pulled the rifle out of the man's hands, ignoring the woman. Turning away from her, he walked purposefully back to Billy. Handing him the rifle, he then bent over and yanked the axe out of the dirt. "Let's get going."

Ethan crawled over to the man's still form and placed his hands on his chest. He wasn't breathing. He sat back and wiped at his face, leaving a streak of blood on his cheek. The woman and child had reached them and were trying to roll the man over, sobbing and wailing his name.

Wesley. His name was Wesley.

CHAPTER 4

OM
North of Idaho Falls

HIS HEAD still felt like someone was using it for a drum. Tom moaned and pressed against his temples, willing it to stop. He had a decent concussion and was still somewhat disoriented, but it didn't matter. He had to keep moving. He had to find Ethan.

The mid-morning sun beat down on him and he was grateful that he at least still had his cowboy hat. Stumbling over a rock, Tom went down to a knee and he stayed there for a moment, gathering himself. He'd been in and out of consciousness the first night after they were attacked. He'd managed to drag himself to the river and then spent half of the next day there, cleaning out the flesh wound on his right shoulder and rehydrating. He knew he might eventually regret drinking so much unfiltered water, but his options were limited.

Tom looked idly over at a man and woman walking by on the

other side of the freeway, likely intentionally giving him a wide berth. He had a week's growth of beard, an oozing wound over his eye, bruising on his forehead, a bandaged arm, and dirty clothes. Given his size, it was a reasonable assumption that he was a potential threat. He staggered to his feet. "Hello!"

The woman moved closer to the man, who glanced at Tom and kept walking.

They were on the same open stretch of Interstate 15 that he and Ethan traveled two days earlier, just north of Idaho Falls. Tango, Ethan's horse, left a distinct track that Tom had spotted several times going south, so he was certain they'd also come back through this way. However, confirmation that Ethan was *on* the horse would be a relief. "Please, I just want to ask a question. Have you seen two men and a teenage boy on horses?"

While Tom had encountered several bikers and a couple of people on horseback, he was hoping the larger group of horses would stand out.

The man ignored Tom and the woman shook her head. "Sorry. No, we haven't. We just left Idaho Falls a couple of hours ago. You...shouldn't go there." The man pulled at her and they hurried away, their arms laden with duffel bags.

Tom had no intention of entering the city, and could only pray that he'd pick their trail back up on the other side, on the same highway. He was already half a day behind and at a huge disadvantage being on foot and without much for gear. The convicts had left his pack on his back, but dumped the contents out and taken his clothes and water bottle. A small fire-making kit and some other essentials were still in the zippered pockets.

By the time he'd been steady enough to walk back up the trail to the rest stop, Tom figured close to twenty hours had passed since the ambush. They likely stopped and slept at some point, but he was still going to be far behind. He broke into an abandoned semi in the parking lot and found two empty bottles of water and a decent first-aid kit in the glove box.

The gunshot turned out to be a flesh wound, although it could have used a few stitches. After some carefully applied butterfly Band-Aids, antibiotic ointment, and a few Advil, Tom filled the water bottles at the river and then set out. He didn't make it more than a few miles before he got dizzy and had to stop. He woke up hours later, in the dark, confused. It happened one more time during the night, but hopefully, the episodes were behind him.

The terrain was basically flat, so Tom could see the ominous dark haze hanging over Idaho Falls from far away. As he got closer, it looked like the fires had only grown in size. Since the Snake River wasn't far from the highway, more tents and obvious camps appeared along its banks as he neared the city. In the day and a half since he'd last been through, the outskirts were beginning to look more like a warzone. It was time to find another road, and now that he was on foot, he'd like to give the main part of the city an even wider berth.

His map was gone, but Tom remembered that the airport was just ahead and there should be a side road that went around it. It meant adding some time to his journey, though in addition to the fires, the streets were guaranteed to be dangerous and he was unarmed and certainly not at a hundred percent.

When Tom finally saw the obviously named "Airport Vantage Road" sign he was happy to leave the highway and find some shade. It was another scorching day and he was trying not to drink all of his water. The tree-lined road would have been idyllic, if not for the wreckage of at least two planes strewn about.

It wasn't a huge airport, and Tom was at the farthest corner of the airstrip, and yet the impact of the flash was still painfully apparent. The terminal in the distance was in smoldering ruins, and half of the trees on the street were sheared in half, a clear indication of the chaos that ensued when the planes lost power. He turned his attention to the cars parked along the street that were barely recognizable, and he wondered how many of them had been occupied. Half of the houses on the other side of the road showed various levels of damage, and a few of them had burned to the ground. Once a serene neighborhood, it now served as a stark example of how so much was lost in an instant.

Thankfully, the road was still passable on foot—and it wasn't like turning around was much of an option. Tom gritted his teeth and did his best to ignore the bodies mixed in with the debris. One of the planes was mostly intact and must have dropped from the sky either right after take-off or just before landing. The front end of it had snapped a telephone pole in half before becoming embedded in another, but the back half was basically unscathed. As Tom passed the open door of the small passenger plane, he told himself that the occupants would have been okay and made it out. It made ignoring the rest of it a little easier.

Two miles farther, he was beyond the fields and entering a district full of churches, a park, and a school. More people were out milling around, most of them with distant, detached expressions. A woman sat sobbing on a park bench and people passed by without stopping. There wasn't anything anyone could do.

The lack of running water and working sewers was more apparent the closer he got to the densely populated areas. It was a smell Tom compared to an over-used outhouse permeating the air. Garbage was piling up outside the buildings and he was constantly swatting at flies.

Tom avoided eye contact with anyone he got close enough to see clearly. Mixed in with what were mostly average-looking suburban dwellers were those with a more menacing demeanor. They had a desperate air about them and, armed or not, were dangerous. He could hear gunshots coming from the city, and yelling and screaming randomly echoed from nearby. The sense of unease was palpable as the number of people present increased, a foreboding like nothing he'd ever experienced before.

At the small school, Tom made a detour. He was too slow and if he ever hoped to catch up to Ethan, he needed to find some kind of transport. A car was too much to hope for, but a bike would improve his chances tenfold. At the back of the school, he spotted a family that had pitched a tent under some trees on the playground. The man lifted his toddler-aged son into the air, eliciting a childish giggle from him, and Tom smiled at them, reminded of better times.

Following the back wall of the two-story brick building, he finally came upon what he was looking for: a long bike rack. To his surprise, there was actually a ten-speed there. It was rusted, had a low tire, and was too small for him, but he would happily use it.

Before peddling away, Tom paused and looked at the back doors of the school. One of them was open several inches and as he thought about what could be inside, his stomach grumbled. It had been almost two days since he'd eaten anything. His goal was to get to Ed and Marnie's by the next day, but part of his weakness was likely due to a lack of calories.

The school had to have a cafeteria and although school had been out for the summer when the flash hit, they probably kept some nonperishables stocked. Maybe he'd get lucky and it wasn't looted yet. Tom got off the bike and approached the doors cautiously, looking behind him. The family was out of view and aside from a couple of people walking by at a distance, there wasn't anyone obviously paying attention, so he went inside.

It was an entrance to the auditorium, so aside from the doors, there wasn't much ambient light. Tom quickly crossed the murky room, his footsteps echoing much too loudly. On the far side, he was relieved to find a hallway with large windows at the far end. It didn't take long to find the cafeteria, with its stacked tables and chairs. Tom leaned against the doorjamb as another wave of dizziness momentarily blurred his vision. During the brief spell of disorientation, he thought he could hear children laughing and chairs scraping against the floor. Rubbing his head to clear it, Tom forced himself from the childhood memory and back into the present. He had to find some food.

Blinking rapidly, he used the steel countertop to help steady himself as he walked into the back work area. He avoided the walk-in freezer door, and went for the dry storage area next to it.

"Bingo!" he murmured as he shrugged his backpack off and unzipped it. Reaching for a box of granola bars, he was too distracted to hear the stealthy steps coming up behind him.

"Ugh!" Tom grunted as someone slammed into his back, and tried to wrap him up. Although surprised, it was immediately obvious that his attacker was smaller than him and he easily counterbalanced the assault.

Planting his right foot forward, Tom shoved backwards and slammed the man into the shelving. When the arms around him loosened, he stepped out of the embrace and spun around, lashing out at the same time with his left fist. There was a solid, satisfying connection and cartilage crunched under his knuckles. A rage welled up in Tom that he hadn't felt since he was a teen. Raw emotion that he'd spent years learning how to keep in check, but was now dangerously close to escaping.

"Stop!" a woman shrieked. Footsteps rushed towards them. "Please. We're just trying to protect the food for everyone."

Tom sucked in ragged mouthfuls of hot, stagnant air, struggling to breathe through the adrenaline rush. He still held his fist above him, poised to pummel the man on the ground at his feet. He took a step back.

"Please," the woman repeated. It was the one from the tent on the playground. She knelt next to the man and propped his shoulders, helping him to sit. Behind her, a small boy peeked around the counter, his eyes round with fear.

Tom felt bile rising in his throat and coughed once to force it back. His field of vision widened as his head cleared and his heartrate slowed. He looked at the box of granola bars, still clasped in his right hand.

"We're both teachers here," the man croaked and spit blood onto the floor. Slowly, he got to his feet. "This food belongs to the people who live here. Not you."

Tom dropped the box into his pack and zipped it up without comment. Slinging it over his good shoulder, he sidestepped the couple. He offered a smile to the small boy, but it only caused him to run crying to his mom. He kept forgetting how his face must look. "I only need enough for a day," he offered by way of an explanation. "I'm leaving. You don't need to worry about me. Sorry…about your face."

When neither of them said anything in response or tried to stop him, Tom made his way back outside. The heat was stifling, but he looked up gratefully at the sky, glad to be in the sun. Shading his eyes, he squinted and studied the horizon to the south. The normally dark blue color had an odd haze to it. It was something other than the smoke he'd grown accustomed to, and was instead a weird, orange hue. Shrugging, he took out a granola bar and jogged back to the bike rack. Relieved that the ten-speed was still there, he jammed the food in his mouth before riding away as fast as possible.

The small bike was awkward, but it would still more than double his traveling speed. He steered with his good arm while finishing off the bar, forcing the calories down. The granola was dry in his mouth and he was having a hard time swallowing it. What had he become? He'd just broken a man's nose over a box of snacks.

"You have to survive," he said aloud. For his son. And while Tom knew that in all fairness he'd been attacked and was just defending himself, he also knew what he was capable of. He'd do whatever was necessary to get to Ethan, and God help those men when he did.

CHAPTER 5

USSELL
Randolph, Utah

RUSSELL STOPPED behind a burnt-out gas station and quickly assessed his surroundings. The sign just outside of the small town had said "Welcome to Randolph, Population 488. The friendliest town in the West". He suspected it was less so since the event, based on the number of buildings left standing on the three-block long main street. It most likely started with an explosion at the pumps and quickly spread from there. The crispy corpses in the vehicle straddling the pump island attested to it.

According to a sign on the other side of the freeway, in two days he'd traveled thirty-three miles. Russell thought he could walk faster than that. There were still several hours left before the sun went down, but...he needed a better mode of transportation.

Turning to look at a small store still standing on the other side of the alley, Russell wiped at his forehead. He didn't like to sweat, but had little choice in the blazing heat of the day. The long-sleeved prison guard shirt didn't help. He'd like to swap it out for something else, as well as find some other essentials, and the store was likely his only option for another day or two.

"Randolph, let's see how nice you are," Russell purred as he stepped over some rubble. The few people he'd passed on the street on the way through didn't look very accommodating, and they hadn't spoken to him. He pushed at the glass door and grinned when a bell chimed over the entrance.

"We're closed!" A man barked from the gloomy recesses of the building.

Russell wrinkled his nose at an unpleasant smell and then cleared his throat. "Hello?" he made sure to have a waver in his voice. "I'm an employee from the state hospital, just trying to make it home to my family." He cleared his throat again, feigning nervousness, as he edged his way down an aisle, then grinning at the lack of response when the man mistakenly assessed him as not a threat. "I'd appreciate any help you could offer me. I don't need much and I can pay."

"I don't have much and what's left isn't for sale. You'll need to move along."

Russell took care to avoid stepping on a bag of chips on the ground as he rounded a tall stack of canned goods. There was a candle burning on the back counter, but it was still dark enough for him to avoid being seen.

"Hello?" The store owner moved out from behind the counter and walked cautiously towards where he'd last heard Russell. "I said you need to leave."

Russell was enjoying himself so much that he considered dragging the game of hide-and-seek out for a while longer, but there were too many people outside to risk it. Instead, he slid stealthily behind the older man and brought a can of soup down onto his head with such force that he collapsed mid-stride.

"Now, that wasn't very friendly of you," Russell admonished, dropping the can onto his chest with a dull thud. It sounded like the man was still breathing, though he didn't care one way or the other. Removing his backpack, he quickly went about seeing what the town of Randolph had to offer.

Less than an hour later, he was a mile out of town and sipping on a lime sports drink. Not his favorite flavor, but it couldn't be helped. His bag was rather full with random supplies after his binge shopping, and it further compelled him to reassess how he was traveling.

There were a few farms scattered across the wastelands and he could probably find himself a horse, but it wasn't his first choice. He'd never gotten along well with animals. They seemed to have the ability to see into his soul, where others couldn't.

There was a little yellow house not far ahead, with a barn about the same size. Maybe he'd find a bike in there. Whistling, he picked up his pace and pulled a map out of his back pocket to study again while he walked. It was a good find and he'd almost missed it. The rack of postcards, hand-made greeting cards, and local roadmaps was situated off to the side of the entrance of the store, and if he hadn't bumped into it on the way out, he'd still be wondering where, exactly, he was.

It was a long way to Mercy, Montana. Russell didn't mind. The world was suddenly a new landscape to twist and shape into whatever reality he chose.

He paused next to an abandoned sedan and, after a brief debate, pulled at the open driver's door and reached in and popped the trunk. Just as he'd thought, nothing useful was left behind, except maybe... Russell grunted with the effort of pulling up the floor to reveal the spare tire. He smiled and started whistling again as he popped the two-foot long lug wrench from its bracket.

Hefting the heavy tool, he turned back to the yellow house. He certainly didn't plan on carrying it for long, but it would come in handy if anyone was home.

Russell ignored the house and went straight to the barn. The rusted hinges squeaked when he pulled on the large double doors, but opened easily enough. Inside was a literal treasure trove when it came to what one might look for when trying to survive the apocalypse.

"Huh," Russell grunted, stepping inside. It was a large, rather open space with a high ceiling and dirt floor. The barn doors allowed enough light in so that he could turn in a circle and take in all the gear he had to choose from. The owner had been so kind as to carefully sort his shelves, with yard tools and home supplies all on one wall, while hunting and camping gear filled the other.

He stepped up to a box advertising a two-man tent and ran a finger along it. A tractor occupied the majority of floor space; on the far side, against the back wall, were several bikes. Two kids', one woman's ten-speed, and a man's mountain bike. An American flag was tacked to wall above them, one of the white stripes painted blue. Russell was absorbing the meaning when the door banged open behind him.

"I'd suggest you come out so I can see you." The man's voice was full of authority and left no room for argument.

Russell carefully set the lug wrench on the back of the tractor before stepping out from behind it, hands raised. As he expected, the large, middle-aged man facing him was dressed in a police uniform. The officer had his service revolver aimed at him so Russell took a couple of quick steps to close the distance between them.

"That's far enough," the officer said evenly. He frowned as he took in Russell's attire. "You from the mental hospital?"

"Well, yes sir, Officer...Rogers," Russell answered, reading the man's badge. "I only worked there for a month, but I stuck around as long as I could. Everyone else left."

The deputy relaxed his stance slightly without lowering the gun. He tilted his head as he continued to study Russell. He was obviously a man with strong instincts.

Russell kept his hands splayed out at his sides in a placating gesture. "I apologize for not going to the door, but I'm afraid the last one I knocked on nearly earned me an extra hole in my head." He laughed lightly and shrugged. "All I'm looking for is a sleeping bag. It's been a while since I had to sleep on the ground." He smiled. "Do you know what the heck happened? I've asked five people and gotten five different answers."

Deputy Rogers lowered the gun a foot and turned slightly to point at the camping gear. "I've got—"

Russell grabbed the wrench sitting inches from his hand and in one swift movement, brought it down on the man's right fore-arm. The Glock clattered to the ground and the deputy staggered forward a step, his face contorted in pain and shock. Not stop-ping the motion, Russell whipped the tool back around and it connected with the officer's right temple.

He could have left then. Taken what he wanted and left Deputy Rogers unconscious on the floor, to be found later by the ten-speed riding woman. But for all of the lives Russell had extinguished, he'd never used a gun. He picked the Glock up and felt the weight of it. The power.

He knelt next to the man at his feet and studied him for a moment. The rise and fall of his chest, the blood pooling under his cheek, slowly being absorbed into the dirt. Russell carefully pressed the Glock against Deputy Roger's spine, at the base of his skull, and pulled the trigger. The result was immediate and somewhat unsatisfying. There was a reason he'd never killed with a gun before. It was so...impersonal.

Minutes later, Russell slowly buttoned his new shirt, hoping the small bloodstain on the back would blend into the dark brown. He pocketed Tim Ridgeway's nametag before readjusting his new badge.

"I always thought I looked like a Rogers."

CHAPTER 6

$\mathcal{C}$HLOE
Outskirts of Mercy, Montana

THE SUN WAS JUST SLIDING behind the mountains as Chloe
stepped off the trail and into a gravel trailhead parking lot. She
staggered past two empty vehicles with forest passes hanging in
their windshields and stopped in front of a large brown sign.

"Mercy Loop Trail," Chloe read out loud, smiling broadly. "I
can't believe we finally made it."

"Let's hope the people in town are doing better than we are,"
Bishop said, moving up next to her. He turned to address the rest
of the group. "We have no idea what's happened. They may not
be as happy as we are about us reaching their town."

Chloe's brow furrowed as his words sank in. She hadn't even
considered that. She'd been so focused on getting to Mercy that she
didn't think about whether they'd be welcome. From their camp
halfway down the mountain the night before, they had been able to

confirm there still weren't any obvious working electric lights or moving vehicles. It looked like two structural fires were still smoldering, but otherwise the main part of the tiny town appeared intact.

"Why wouldn't they help us?" Crissy asked. She'd removed her heavy trail pack and was sitting on it. Her face was painfully red, and small blisters dotted the tip of her nose.

"Because if all of their electronics are wiped out and they've been cut off for the past five days, they might be getting pretty desperate," Ripley explained. The attractive young woman was barely recognizable from when the trek had started. Her company shirt was dirty, sweat-stained, and torn from when she'd fallen. Her lower legs were covered in scratches from the unplanned, unmaintained trail, and her long brown hair was a matted mess. The intense UV rays had also burned her face, and she'd broken out in fever blisters on her lips so it was painful for her to even talk.

"Why should they be desperate?" Trevor countered, setting his pack next to Crissy's and leaning his back against hers for support. They'd been forced to give him another EpiPen the night before after a second allergic episode and the teen was left weakened and pale. "Living out here in the middle of nowhere, I bet they lose power all the time in the winter. Five days isn't that long."

"This isn't just five days without power," Chloe replied, kicking at a rock. It was discouraging to reach their goal, only to realize they might yet face another obstacle. She just wanted to drink a gallon of water, eat a burger, and sleep in a soft bed for twenty-four hours. She pushed her short black hair back from her face, thinking of how the purple tips had seriously lost any of their original appeal. "If it was only that, they'd be running generators. But they're not."

"No, they're not." Bishop's voice was ominous.

"Which means they've truly been without *any* power for five days. So, no refrigerators, no running water—"

"And no cars," Trevor interrupted Chloe. She didn't think it was possible, but his face took on a paler hue. "Do you think all of their, like...electronics and stuff got fried, too, like our radios and phones? I mean, yeah, of course they must have, but man. Seriously. This is really messed up."

"How are we going to get home?" Crissy looked panicked.

Bishop put his hands up. "Woah. Let's not get ahead of ourselves. Like I said, we don't know what the situation is. It might not be that bad. Or, it could be limited to this area, and there's already help here or on the way. I just want us all to be aware that we shouldn't waltz into town asking to be taken care of. If they're already struggling to fend for themselves, five strangers will be a low priority."

Chloe nodded and fought against a fresh wave of anxiety when she imagined how they would look, walking into town in their dirty clothes and unwashed hair. They were a pretty rough-looking group at the moment. What were they supposed to do if no one would help them? She was almost out of water and down to her last couple of snacks.

Chloe looked up at the darkening sky and saw the first of the stars twinkling to life. She found it reassuring to see that something hadn't changed, but then she noticed the flickering of the northern lights chasing the last of the sunlight away and her anxiety increased. Turning from the odd display, she instead studied the thick evergreens surrounding them. It still felt like they were a long way from civilization, although Bishop estimated it was less than five miles to downtown Mercy. Birds called to each other in the twilight and the aroma of warmed pine needles completed the confusing masquerade of normalcy. Chloe glanced at the abandoned cars and then up again at the brightening ribbons of purple and red to remind herself that things *weren't* normal. She wondered if they ever would be.

"Come on." Ripley tugged at Crissy and Trevor, eliciting moans. "It's already late. I'd like to try and make our arrival as undramatic as possible."

Trevor stood wearily and helped Crissy up. In spite of everything he'd endured, he was still remaining optimistic and supportive to his friends. Chloe thought about how she'd misjudged him as she watched him lift Crissy's pack for her. She'd always considered herself a good judge of character, and it made her wonder how many other people she'd been wrong about.

They made their way out to a road that seemed to be heading in the general direction of town, but they didn't make it more than a quarter mile before Chloe heard the distinct clopping of a horse coming toward them.

"Hello!" Ripley called out before the animal came into view. "We don't want to startle your horse."

The clip-clop slowed and then horse and rider appeared as they rounded a bend on the steeply slanted road. Chloe saw it was a middle-aged woman with thick black hair pulled back in a ponytail. She sat astride the horse in a way that left no doubt she'd spent a lifetime doing it. The woman was also holding a rifle.

"Name's Carl Kingston," Bishop said, stepping forward. "The kids call me Bishop. I'm one of the leaders and co-founder for Trek Thru Trouble. It's a program—"

"I know what it is," the woman interrupted. "I donated to it last year. You and your crew are a long way off course. Your office is almost a hundred miles that way." She gestured toward the shadowy mountains at her back.

"We were on the Lewis and Clark trail when the...um, light happened," Bishop explained. "Vehicles at our drop points didn't work. Mercy was the closest civilization we could reach with the supplies we had." He pointed at the rest of their group. "This is Ripley, I mean Emily, and three of our kids. The rest of us got split up, unfortunately. We're hoping the other four will make it here in a few days."

The woman shifted in her saddle and then lowered the rifle, resting it across her lap. Chloe let out a breath she didn't realize she was holding and began breathing again.

"Name's Sandy Miller. I apologize for the unfriendly greeting. Things are a bit restless right now and, no offense, but you're looking a little ragged."

Crissy started crying. "Do you have a phone?" She wiped at her face and then winced when her tears got into an open blister. "I really want to call my mom."

It was rapidly getting darker, but Chloe was still able to see the change in Sandy's demeanor as her features softened. "How long have you been out there?" She directed the question to Bishop.

"Seven days." Bishop removed his ballcap and took a small step towards Sandy. "Please. We have no idea what's going on. If you could help us get some water and information, I can work on getting these kids reunited with their parents and we'll be on our way."

Sandy shifted in her saddle again and looked at each of them, ending with Chloe. Chloe met her gaze and was disturbed to see tears welling in the older woman's eyes.

"I'm afraid it isn't going to be that easy. Come on." Sandy urged her horse into motion. "Follow me. My ranch is just a mile up the road here. We'll get you cleaned up."

Chloe was so utterly exhausted that she barely noticed the impressive arched entrance to the Miller ranch, made of huge raw timbers. A half-moon and the northern lights provided enough illumination to reveal the A-frame log home, complete with wrap-around porch and a massive barn not far behind it. It was all tucked on a plateau of one of the mountains that encircled Mercy. Acres of fenced pasture surrounded them, all bordered by thick evergreen woods nestled below sharp, jagged mountain peaks that rose above them in the near distance.

"Wow," Trevor whistled. "My mom would love this."

"My son Tom runs the ranch now, but he's...not here at the moment." Sandy gracefully dismounted her horse and tied him to a hitching post near the home's entrance. "I'll get you all settled and then tend to Skywalker." She ran a hand down Skywalker's silky neck before leading the way up the wide steps.

Chloe gratefully removed her pack and shoes and set her gear next to everyone else's on the porch before entering the house. Sandy was in the process of going around the large open room, lighting candles. It revealed a river-rock fireplace that filled half of one wall. Chloe remembered seeing something similar in a ski lodge once, and was fascinated with how much work must have gone into creating it. Over-stuffed leather couches occupied the center of the room, arranged in front of the hearth. In the soft candlelight, Chloe couldn't see much else, but got a strong sense of history and family. Sandy waved a hand at them, encouraging them to move further into the room.

"Please, sit down." Sandy chose to perch on the edge of the fireplace, but immediately stood again and began pacing, looking nervous. "I have a lot to tell you."

CHAPTER 7

ATTY
Mercy, Montana

"I DON'T KNOW what to do, Patty." Dr. Melissa Olsen was seated at a small table across from Patty. A floor lamp and two candles offered just enough light in the doctor's office to see by. The second of the town's two diesel generators grumbled from outside in the alley. "I should have admitted this days ago—I don't have nearly enough help and we need to move to a bigger building."

Patty looked down at the list of names on the papers under her hands. She'd come by to get the latest reports from Melissa, and it was immediately clear that they needed to make some changes. Most of her initial patients had either died or gone home, but she still had several housed in the three small exam rooms. Even at the late hour, six people were crowded into the small waiting room out front. From the confines of Melissa's office, Patty could hear sobbing and moaning, mixed in with several conversations. A twinge of guilt made her take a heavy breath.

"Melissa, I'm sorry." Patty reached across the table and took the younger woman's hands. If she and Caleb had had a daughter, she'd be about her age. "I should have stopped back in sooner. I made an assumption that you had enough hands in here and I didn't consider the ongoing health issues that are coming up."

"It's okay," Melissa said quickly. "None of us could have known. Matt and Em have been great," she added, referring to the one nurse in town and her normal medical assistant. "But I need more."

Patty flipped the top sheet over and looked at the second and third. "Three more deaths? I thought there were only two."

"Sheriff Waters found Mrs. Dutton a couple of hours ago," Melissa explained. "I gave him a list of patients to check on for me. She was an insulin-dependent diabetic and had a hard time getting around. I should have thought of her sooner. I should have—"

"Don't," Patty interrupted. "Don't blame yourself. You can't. It's impossible for you to be responsible for everyone."

Melissa nodded. "I know that, except it doesn't make the guilt go away."

Patty stood and placed her hands on the table, looking stoically at her friend. "Melissa, right now we can't afford the luxury of feeling guilty. These first few weeks are going to be the worst, but I strongly believe that if we can make it through them, we'll be okay. Now, tell me how I can help. What do you need?"

"The cafeteria at the school."

"Really?" It wasn't what Patty had expected.

Melissa shoved another paper across the table at her and Patty recognized a rough floorplan of the high school. "I'll treat it like a mass casualty triage. Frankly, I was surprised this wasn't included in the disaster plan."

Patty took the drawing and was impressed at how organized it was. "Do we have this many cots?"

Shaking her head, Melissa pointed at the drawing. "Turn it over. I list the supplies and ideas of where to get them. The fire department has a few, as do the police. I have a few, too. I suggest putting a call out, since I'm sure there are some people with camping cots that would work. I can use the cafeteria space and utilities to a limited degree with the generator. A couple of the volunteers in the fire department are EMTs and they've agreed to work a couple of shifts a week, but I'll need more."

Patty sat back down and tipped her head questioningly at the doctor. "Melissa, this looks good and you know you have my full support, but do you really need this much?"

Right on cue, Em stuck her head into the office and looked apologetically at Melissa. "Sorry, Doc, I think we've got another dehydration case. Pretty severe."

"Enough to warrant one of the last bags of fluid?" Melissa asked, her face a mask of concern.

"Maybe." Em looked at Patty and smiled. "Hey, Mayor. Didn't you use to be a nurse? Wanna start a line?"

Patty grimaced at the girl who didn't look any older than eighteen. "I could, but I don't think your patient would appreciate it. It's been nearly twenty years since I did much nursing."

Em shrugged and turned back to Melissa. "And two more patients just came in. Look like the others."

Patty watched the door close and then blinked at Melissa. "What was that about?"

"The reason I need so many beds," Melissa answered. She rubbed at her eyes and Patty noticed how pronounced the bags under them were getting. "I'm pretty sure it's radiation poisoning."

Patty blanched. She'd had a mild headache for two days but had been writing it off as stress and lack of sleep.

"So far, it's primarily infants, the elderly, and those with compromised immune systems." Melissa pushed yet another sheet of paper at Patty. "I've made a list of the symptoms; it lines up with everything I've read about gamma radiation. But," she urged, "I think it qualifies as mild. Especially since it was five days after the event before anyone started complaining."

"I've had a headache," Patty said, her voice hoarse. "Caleb, too."

"Could be radiation," Melissa confirmed. "Or it could be from you pushing yourself way too hard, Patty. You're almost seventy. It's ten at night and I'll bet you have hours of things left to check off your list for the day. When was the last time you slept in your bed?"

Patty ignored the question. "What are you able to do about them? The patients with radiation poisoning."

Melissa leaned back in her seat and let Patty get away with the side-stepping. "In a normal world, I'd send them to Helena for hospitalization, where they'd get IV fluids, anti-nausea medication, anti-diarrhea meds, and, depending on bloodwork, other supportive measures for their internal organs. However, given the current circumstances, it depends on how severe it is. I have a very limited amount of medicine. This is set up as a small clinic. I *do* have all of those things stocked up and even quite a bit of extra fluids because I like to be prepared, but it isn't nearly enough."

"Homeopathic remedies?" Patty suggested.

Melissa smiled. "More like over-the-counter, though that's a good suggestion that I'll look into. The store and even most people stock antacids and Pedialyte. Sports drinks that have electrolytes are also beneficial. Basically, I'm doing everything I can to keep them hydrated without using IV fluids, but I've already had to resort to it with a handful of patients. Normally, I think it would be a fairly easy recovery but I'm worried about our more fragile population, especially once I run out, if this goes on for too long."

Em poked her head in again and Melissa stood. "I better get back out there."

"I'll talk to Sheriff Waters and Fire Chief Martinez," Patty promised, standing with her. "We'll move you to the school tomorrow and find some more help for you, too."

Melissa gave a tired smile. "Thank you. We've been lucky, you know," she added as they walked out together to the front door. "So far, things have been manageable for the most part. That could change quickly."

Patty spent several years working in a busy emergency department and she knew exactly what Melissa meant. And she was right. Walking out onto the dark street, she quickly dug the flashlight out of her sweatshirt pocket and snapped it on. She'd been living out in the country for years now and had never been fearful of the dark, but the past few days she found herself panicking in it.

Quickly making her way down Main Street to City Hall, she made a point of saying hello to the few people she encountered along the way. While the town meeting and barbeque had created a sense of solidarity and helped to calm the rising tension, things were a long way off from being okay. They had only just begun to set some of the plans into motion, let alone adequately meeting everyone's needs.

She entered the meeting hall, which had officially become their center of operations. Caleb was seated at the far end of the large circular oak table with Gary, who had become a surprisingly strong cornerstone in the town's efforts to recover.

"Do you really think six horses will be enough?" Gary was asking. "And only two stations? Why don't we do three stations, here...here...and here. Then, with eight horses, we can complete a circuit to Helena in one day, instead of two."

Caleb frowned and sat back from the table, running his hands over his head. Patty recognized the gesture and readied herself to intervene. "I already told you, Gary," he said with a heavy sigh. "The horses can't be run that hard! There wouldn't be any benefit to it. One station here in town, and one at the halfway mark. I've studied the Pony Express and I'm telling you, this is the best way to do it."

Gary noticed Patty first and waved her over. "What do you think?"

She held her hands up to fend off the request. "Sorry, uh-uh. I have enough on my plate already. I'll leave the whole Pony Express idea to you two. Although, I'm sure it's a brilliant idea. All I know is that it ran for a while during the mid-1800s and the only reason it stopped was because of the telegraph and rail lines, both things we don't have at the moment. Speaking of which, have the scouts gotten back yet?"

Early the day before, two volunteers had set out for Helena on horseback. The mission was two-fold: to find out the state of the road and city, and to see how long the journey would take. A few residents had made it back to Mercy on foot, after being stranded after the flashpoint. One of them had come all the way from Helena, but they'd left immediately after the event and didn't have much useful information other than it had been total chaos.

Caleb looked concerned. "No, not yet."

"They were going to one of their relatives that lives on the outskirts," Gary offered. "Hopefully they're just resting for a day before heading back."

Patty tried to gather her thoughts. She had so many different things to work on, but the dull, persistent ache behind her eyes brought Melissa's suggestion back to mind. She rubbed at the low throbbing in her temples, giving a slight groan and wishing she could be at home in bed already.

"Are you okay?" Caleb rose and made his way to where Patty was leaning against the table. "We should go home."

Patty gently shrugged away from the arm he was trying to put around her shoulders and turned instead towards the whiteboard stationed at the back of room. "In a minute."

Walking on legs that felt like lead weights, Patty forced herself to go pick up a red marker and face the board. She rubbed at the numbers with the palm of her hand and then changed the population of Mercy from 655 to 652.

CHAPTER 8

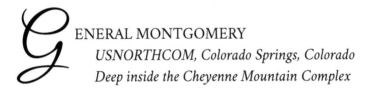

ENERAL MONTGOMERY
USNORTHCOM, Colorado Springs, Colorado
Deep inside the Cheyenne Mountain Complex

Four-star USAF General Andrew Montgomery sat staring at the latest communication reports from his executive assistant. It wasn't anything good. The crease between his brows deepened, eliciting the iconic expression that caused fear in most of his staff. Grunting, he stood slowly, and tugging at his uniform jacket, approached what he was coming to think of as "the wall".

A monstrous three-by-six-foot map of the world was hung front and center in the command room, per his instructions. It had taken two days to track down the large, color-coded tacks he'd requested and listening to Colonel Walsh, he made it sound as if he'd risked his life for it.

"Sir," Colonel Walsh began with some trepidation.

General Montgomery paused with his hand mid-air, and turned to look at his executive assistant. "What is it, Kelly?" He was the only member of his staff whom he ever dropped the formalities with. The younger man was one of a handful who didn't buckle under the general's iron will.

Kelly looked down at his feet. "Still no further contact with the White House. It's been two days now, sir." He gestured at the green tack marking Washington, DC. "It's time."

The general knew he wasn't only referring to the color-coding. As he exchanged the green for a red pin, the ventilation system kicked on, echoing deep within the bowels of Cheyenne Mountain.

Five days earlier, he'd been in a meeting at Peterson Air Force Base when the gamma-ray burst hit. His office was a room full of windows with mountain views and plenty of fresh air. Now, he'd never know it was ten at night, if not for the ticking of the clock on the wall. He tugged at his collar. The general had never considered himself claustrophobic, but having two thousand feet of granite looming over your head can change a man.

Peterson Base had some very limited shielding against the EMP, so they were able to establish a line of communication with enough resources the first day to determine what the event was, and that compelled them to evacuate NORAD and USNORTHCOM to the Cheyenne Mountain Complex, ten miles away. Up until then, it had been on a warm stand-by, although over the past few years hundreds of millions had been spent to move their communication equipment to the mountain bunker due to it being completely shielded against any electromagnetic pulse.

USNORTHCOM was a joint command, and while General Montgomery was the commander, he knew the other joint staff weren't all going to agree with his next move, especially Deputy Commander Vice Admiral Welling. However, the reason he'd been put in charge was because those in power knew he'd be able to make the types of decisions others couldn't.

General Montgomery cleared his throat. "Issue a general statement announcing the confirmation of the death of our President, Vice President, Speaker of the House, President Pro Tempore, Secretary of the State, Secretary of the Treasury, Secretary of Defense, and the Attorney General." He turned then to look at Colonel Kelly Walsh. "Etcetera, etcetera for the cabinet. You know the rest of the names."

"Yes, sir."

"Then make it known that I recognize that with the leaders of the civilian government either dead or missing, I am the highest-ranking military officer known to be alive. Therefore, I hereby declare martial law, and take governing control of the US military and the remaining citizens of the United States of America."

Colonel Walsh wrung his hands nervously. He'd effectively just become the executive assistant to the president. "I'll have the statement issued immediately."

General Montgomery turned back to his map. A swath of black made a wide, diagonal trail northeast across it, marking the military bases that never made contact. To either side of that were bands of red, highlighting either bases or other points of communication in the initial days that had since gone silent after reports of radiation sickness. In only five days, different zones were becoming clearly defined and the small amount of land unaffected was terrifying.

Essentially, the northwest portion of the United States, Alaska, most of Canada, Australia, and Greenland were spared. But that only related to the immediate effects of the gamma-ray burst. In the coming days and months, there would be many other hardships to conquer.

The general's hand hovered over a black pin on the Greek island of Crete. His son was stationed there at Souda Bay, along with his daughter-in-law and two grandchildren. He would never see them again.

"Once the statement is released, I'm naming you the Director of FEMA," Andrew stated with his back still facing his assistant and friend. He knew Kelly would balk against the assignment.

"You can't be serious!" Kelly moved up alongside the general so he'd be forced to look at him. "With everything we have yet to get done here? You want me out running around setting up camps?"

General Montgomery thumbed through the papers in his hand until he found the one he wanted. Holding it out to Kelly, he raised his eyebrows. "Out of ten FEMA offices, only three are operational. Region Eight is less than seventy miles from here in Denver. I'll authorize you to use our one working helo to fly there. One week, Kelly." He leaned toward the shorter man for emphasis, his large trim frame hovering inches from him. "By the time you start organizing it will be one week without any intervention on the state or federal level. The FEMA state caches must be accessed and deployed, and I need boots on the ground. I'm counting on you to make this happen."

He turned and opened his arms to encompass the world map. "Millions are dead. Hundreds of millions, probably billions by the time this settles. We're looking at around twenty-five percent of our country that's still able to function at some level. If we don't intervene and provide for these survivor's basic needs, this could very well be an extinction level event."

"I'm going to need help with the logistics," Kelly admitted. "While we have a couple of armored vehicles that survived the burst, those aren't going to be of any use beyond our immediate vicinity. Same goes for the helicopter."

General Montgomery sighed. "Come on, Colonel. You don't need me to hold your hand. Coordinate with the other bases and compile a list of your assets and where they are. Include all state and National Guard. Work the problem."

"Right," Kelly replied. He'd worked with General Andrew

Montgomery for over a decade and knew when to simply accept an order. "I included our latest supply numbers in your report. Sorry I got it to you so late, but there was a lot going on today."

Andrew looked down at the papers and again flipped through them. After a moment he looked up, his brows drawn together. "These look great. Over four million gallons of spring-fed water in reserve, and enough diesel and self-charging batteries to power a city twice our size." The Cheyenne complex was comprised of fifteen three-story buildings taking up five acres under the granite mountain, so that was saying a lot. "Why do I get the feeling there's a reason you took the time to point this out?"

Kelly sat down at the large glossy table in the middle of the room and looked up at the general with an apprehensive expression. "There have been several more requests by mountain personnel to allow their family members inside."

"You know that isn't going to happen. Peterson Air Force Base is more than sufficient to accommodate any enlisted families seeking refuge."

Kelly leaned forward and rested his elbows on his knees and simply stared at the general. Andrew knew it was a practiced gesture and was meant to be submissive, but for some reason it caused him further agitation. "What?" he demanded. "What do you expect me to say? You know the regulations as well as I do. The mountain is closed. No one leaves unless under direct order, and no one enters, especially not *family* members!"

"Peterson is being overrun," Kelly pushed. "Colorado Springs is in shambles so people are evacuating and the remaining military personnel at the base can't keep people out without shooting them."

"So, they should shoot them." Andrew closed his eyes as soon as he said it, knowing what the rebuttal would be.

"General, we're talking about women and children. Civilians

only looking for drinkable water and shelter."

"Right." The general pinched the bridge of his nose and took a breath. Kelly was his friend, but he still needed to be mindful of what he said. "Cheyenne Mountain and this command isn't about a limited amount of military personnel and their families surviving. It's about coordinating the rescue and survival of the rest of our country, and we can't allow anything to undermine that mission."

"Like a mutiny."

Andrew's head snapped up at that and he stared hard at Kelly. He took a measured step toward him. "You'd better explain that statement *very* carefully."

Kelly licked his lips. "You've got nearly seven hundred soldiers under this mountain, locked away from their families while the world around them crumbles. Meanwhile, they see a facility capable of housing three times as many people, with enough resources to support them indefinitely. You need to remember that most of the personnel down here were never stationed at the mountain. They haven't been through the lockdown drills. They aren't mentally prepared for this. When their loved ones show up at the gate begging to be let inside only to be turned away, you can't be surprised to hear talk about them threatening to walk away from their commands."

"That's treason," Andrew said quietly while looking again at the black pin on the wall.

"It's a reality." Kelly reached out and took the list of FEMA offices from his commander. "We need to give them something, sir. Without hope, they don't have a reason to care, or to stay."

General Montgomery weighed his options carefully. If he took action now it would be of his own accord, rather than under duress. He could also set a strict precedent. "Perhaps you're right, Colonel. Go ahead and set up one of the empty upper levels of building three as a dormitory. Any immediate family member of mountain personnel may be granted access after being cleared personally by you." He stared evenly at Kelly until the other man looked away. "But let it be known that anyone attempting to leave without proper authorization will be incarcerated."

Colonel Walsh stood then and nodded in understanding. "I'll use the intranet to issue the new orders. Is there anything else?"

The general gave a curt shake of his head. "No, but be sure to include that as a printed document in the morning briefing." While the mountain complex was fully shielded and still had a working intranet, it of course had no outside connections or communication other than by radio. Because of this, he was reluctant to even use the old computer system for anything other than its word processor, and felt a need to retrain his staff on doing things the old-fashioned way. That meant hard copies of everything. Outside of the mountain, that was going to be the new reality for the rest of the survivors.

As the door to the command room closed behind the Colonel, General Montgomery set the days reports back down on his desk and took a deep, slow breath. He was fifty-six years old and had been in the military since he was eighteen. It was the only life he remembered and he believed in the command structure, but he'd never imagined himself in his current position. He didn't know if he was capable of leading his country out of the current darkness that had been thrust upon it.

Tapping at the updated list of communications, he noticed a new civilian contact had been added. Smiling, he grabbed a green tack and went back to "the wall". The only way they were going to endure this was by finding survivors and bringing them all together. By protecting them from themselves. He searched the map for a moment and after locating the small valley deep in Montana, he marked it with the green tack.

"Hello, Mercy, Montana."

CHAPTER 9

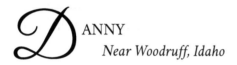

ANNY
Near Woodruff, Idaho

WOODRUFF WASN'T SO MUCH a town as it was a four-way stop with a few buildings lining the road. Though it did have a post office, so it qualified for a name on the map.

"We should stop," Sam called back to Danny. "It's getting too dark to see."

Even though they'd left a couple of hours earlier than normal that morning, they still hadn't gone as far as planned. Danny needed to stop every few miles to rest and finally had to admit halfway through the day that she was struggling. It was going to be another day or two before she regained all of her strength. "Okay," she agreed, uncharacteristically foregoing a fight.

Ominous clouds with an orange hue had built up to the south over the early evening hours and were now blotting out the moon. Danny looked up at the dark skies as they pulled to the side of the road. She'd been wishing for a good storm the past few days while baking under the sun, yet the idea of trying to sleep in it wasn't very appealing.

"Does the tent have a rainfly?" She asked Sam, dropping her pack on the ground next to her bike. Grace ran in a circle around her, excited to be stopping because it meant food and water. Danny was amazed at the resiliency of the golden retriever.

"Yup. But maybe we won't need it." Sam nodded at the dark buildings a block away. "Maybe we can hole up in one of those."

Danny was wary. The last time they'd gone inside a building they'd been shot at. She frowned as she thought about the pharmacy. Sam had managed to find antibiotics and Advil for her, but none of the other meds she'd told him she wanted. Her father had a serious heart condition. She was supposed to bring him his refill during her monthly visit that would normally be that coming weekend. Mercy didn't have a pharmacy, so unless she managed to get some to him, he'd be in trouble sooner rather than later.

"Danny?"

Danny snapped back to the present and blinked at Sam, trying to focus on him in the gathering darkness. She was more exhausted than she realized. "Sorry. Are you sure that's a good idea?"

Lightning cracked across the sky, and instead of the typical white and purple flash, there was an intense orange glow around it. Seconds later, it was followed by ground-shaking thunder.

"Changed my mind." Danny grabbed her gear and righted the bike. "Two to check in to the creepy, hopefully abandoned building." Her joke wasn't far from the truth, and she eyed the weather-beaten structure with some trepidation.

It turned out to be an old mechanic shop, and had likely been vacated long before the flash ever happened. Danny didn't care how decrepit or full of spiderwebs it was. It offered an albeit questionable roof over their heads and an opportunity to sleep without one eye open.

As Sam began spreading out their tarp to lay the sleeping bags on, Danny heard what sounded like a woman sobbing. Pausing with their one working flashlight in her hand, she tilted her head while motioning for Sam to stop. "Do you hear that?"

Sam went back to the front door, which was hanging from its rusted hinges. "Yeah, sounds close. Guess we aren't as alone as we'd hoped."

Danny joined him at the opening as another flash of eerie lightning lit up the street. In the brief moment of illumination, she saw that there were several more buildings a block away. There was obvious fire damage, but some were still intact.

"Please, can you help us?" The voice was coming from a building across the street and sounded like a young woman.

Danny realized she was still holding the flashlight and the woman must have seen it. She hesitated, and then shame surged through her, causing her chest to ache. She was still a paramedic and firefighter. Less than a week ago she would have never even considered turning away from someone begging for help. She stepped out of the shelter of the building.

"Danny," Sam called after her. "Wait. I'll come with you."

Thankful the older man didn't try to stop her, Danny watched as he went back to get the gun. After riding the bike for miles with it tucked into his pants, Sam had broken down and stowed it in the backpack. They'd decided that either finding or making some sort of holster for it was a top priority.

"Hello?" Danny called once they walked together out into the street.

"Yes! Over here!" A woman moved out into the road, waving her arms.

Before Danny could assess the situation, Grace raced forward and then past the woman without slowing. Barking once, she ran in a circle around a wagon on the sidewalk before whimpering and lying down next to it.

Approaching the woman, Danny shone her light on the building and exposed an open, oversized garage door. Inside was a small fire truck, its side panels all open and the contents strewn across the floor. Lowering the light to where Grace lay, she saw a green plastic wagon, and inside was a small boy of about seven years of age. He was conscious, but pale and sweaty. His right leg was propped up on a pillow.

"We live just outside of town," the woman explained. "Jer-imiah fell off the roof. I *told* him not to do it, but he climbed out his second-story window to try and pick some apples from the top of the tree."

Danny offered a small smile to the mom before approaching the wagon. He was wearing shorts and so it was obvious that his right thigh was swollen. Kneeling down, she placed a hand first on top of his bare right foot and then the left. "He has decreased pedal pulses in his right leg," she stated. "When did this happen?"

"About four hours ago," the woman said, kneeling next to Danny. "My name's Sarah. What do decreased pulses mean? Are you a doctor? I thought there might be someone here at the fire station, but I can't find anyone. I didn't know what else to do. His dad...hasn't come back from work since the light happened."

"I'm Danny and this is Sam," Danny said, turning to include Sam. "I'm not a doctor, I'm a paramedic. I'm afraid he might have broken his femur, which is the bone in the thigh. The decreased pulse could be from swelling, but it most likely means that the bone is displaced and causing pressure on the artery that runs near it."

"The femoral artery," Sarah said.

Danny glanced at the woman. "Yes."

"I took some classes years ago to become a Certified Nursing Assistant, and then decided it wasn't for me." Sarah looked at

Danny as another strand of lightning tore across the sky, followed quickly by more thunder. "What can we do?"

Danny stood and began searching through the items on the floor. Whoever had looted the place was thorough. "Sam, could you go get a couple Advil?"

"Oh, I already gave him some," Sarah said quickly. "That, and half a pain pill I had left over from knee surgery last year. He was in so much pain; I hope that was okay."

"It was smart," Danny offered. She tugged at one of the back compartment doors on the truck. The medical bag was gone, of course. However, on the top shelf was an item that could save the boy's life. Fortunately, it wasn't something that anyone would want to steal.

She turned with the two-foot long contraption in her hand. "This is a traction device," Danny said as she approached them. "I can use it to reduce the break and relieve the pressure."

"Will he be okay?" Sarah sobbed, reaching for her sons' hand.

Danny exchanged a look with Sam. "So long as the femoral artery hasn't been cut, he'll be in a lot of pain for a while, but should be okay. We'll improvise a splint for him."

Sarah closed her eyes. "And if the artery is cut?"

Danny positioned herself next to Sarah and took her hand. "Then there isn't anything we can do. Do you still have the other half of that pain pill?" Sarah nodded. "Then give it to him. This is going to hurt."

An hour later, Danny and Sam wearily re-entered the building where their gear still sat, shaking water from their hair. The rain had finally let loose. After successfully reducing Jeremiah's leg and using the traction device as a sort of splint, Sarah had insisted on taking him back home. His thigh was still soft and hadn't shown any signs of filling with blood. Since the pulse in his foot returned, Danny was hopeful the seven-year-old would eventually recover.

"That was pretty amazing," Sam said as they unrolled their sleeping bags. "We've been so busy running and surviving that I'd forgotten what you used to do for a profession. You must have been an incredible medic."

Danny sat on her bedding and stared off into the dark recesses of the open workspace. She was deeply troubled at how easily she'd been able to ignore all of the injured and needy people they'd passed along the way. "I know that it's unrealistic of me to think that I should have stopped and helped more people this past week," she said slowly, her voice sounding hollow. "But it shouldn't have been so...*easy*, Sam. Do you know that I can't even remember them? I'm thinking back over those first days, and aside from the old woman at the airport and the little girl whose mother pulled her away, I can't remember *any* of them."

Sam sat down across from her and after a moment of silence, cleared his throat. "This is about survival. And compartmentalizing. What we've been through...what we've witnessed, is simply too much to process. We're fighters, Danny, so we've done what was necessary to keep going. It doesn't make us bad people."

"Then what does it make us?" She focused on Sam's face then, and saw the same pain she was feeling reflected back in his dark eyes. "I was going to quit."

Sam stared at her quizzically. "Quit what?"

"The department. When I was on the plane, I was on my way back from a job interview in Florida. They'd offered the position to me on the spot and I accepted."

Sam sat quietly and waited for her to continue as the rain drummed on the metal roof.

Danny thought the rain might bring some relief from the heat, but it only added to the humidity. She wiped at her face and then pulled her thick hair up off her neck. "Two years ago, I went on a cruise with my best friend. It was the first vacation I'd had in five years and the last one since this week. Ever since, I've thought about working as an on-board medic, but never really thought it was a move I could realistically make. Then…"

She hesitated. Thunder rolled, underscoring her churning emotions. It was dangerous territory for her. A darkness that threatened to drag her in if she got too close. "I've had problems sleeping for nearly a year. My chief made me talk with a counselor who after one session tried to diagnose me with PTSD. He said it wasn't uncommon for responders to suffer from it."

"Post-traumatic stress disorder," Sam echoed.

Danny nodded. "I wouldn't accept it and never went back. Figured I could work through it on my own." She stopped again and closed her eyes, letting the sounds of the storm envelop her.

"Something happened."

Again, Danny nodded. Sam's gentle prodding was enough to compel her to revisit the event that ultimately made her hit send on the application. Much like the flash, it was too much to process and forced her to shut down part of what made her…her.

"He was five years old." Opening her eyes, she looked at Sam, nostrils flaring. "Five, Sam. He and his mom were on their way home from a family birthday party when a drunk driver hit them. The drunk walked away but we had to use jaws to cut Cody out of the backseat. That was his name. I know, because I still hear his mom screaming it…over, and over again whenever I close my eyes at night."

Grace whined and nudged her hand before lying next to Danny and resting her head in her lap. Danny dug her fingers into the soft hair of the dog's ears, trying to stay grounded in the present.

"He died in my arms, and there wasn't anything I could do for him." A body-racking sob escaped Danny then, and she bent over Grace, embracing the dog.

They stayed that way for several minutes, Sam a silent witness to Danny's release as the storm raged around them. Flashes of lightning glowed a pale green and blue through the cracks in the wall and the glassless window, a reminder that even the sky had been changed by the otherworldly blast. Thunder rumbled a few seconds after each bolt, sounding less like a storm and more like the world itself groaning in agony over how any normalcy had completely vanished.

"There isn't anything I can say to make what you went through any easier," Sam offered when Danny eventually sat back up.

"It isn't supposed to be easy," Danny said hoarsely. She was sure the therapist would say that finally talking about the accident and letting her emotions out would make her feel better, but she only felt...hollow. Sniffing, she wiped at her eyes and struggled to compose herself. "That's the point, Sam. I've had to shut a piece of myself down every time I've experienced something horrific until I don't know what's left. This past week has proven that to me."

Sam reached out and placed a hand on her knee, his face earnest. "Everything you've gone through, Danny, has brought you to this moment. It's prepared you to be the person who I need. Who Grace needs, and your father needs. Who Jerimiah and Sarah needed tonight. You've sacrificed a part of yourself so you can be a survivor when others can't, and will step up and do what needs to be done. There's no shame in that. No guilt."

Danny clung to his words, wanting to believe him. She so desperately wanted to believe him.

CHAPTER 10

OM
Near Blackfoot, Idaho

"Tom."

Tom focused on the voice. He knew he recognized it, but a deep sleep clawed at him, threatening to suck him back under.

"Come on, Tom. Wake up. It's Ed."

Ed. Tom managed to open one eye, but the room was cast in shadows so he forced both open and stared at the old man hovering over him. "I'm awake," he mumbled, pushing himself up onto his elbows. Memories of the night before came rushing back as Tom looked around the familiar family room of the farmhouse.

"That must have been some dream you were havin'," Ed commented. He leaned back from the couch where Tom lay and sat on the coffee table. "You were yelling."

"I don't remember." Tom swung his legs over the side of the couch and sat up. "In fact, I don't remember much from the past couple of days. I barely remember getting here." He gingerly pushed at the swelling over his left eye. He'd had a concussion before, and knew he was suffering through a pretty serious one.

"It's only been about five hours since you got here," Ed explained. He pointed at a window towards the front of the house, where the first hint of morning was dawning. "You showed up on the porch in the middle of the night, shot and confused, looking like you'd been worked over pretty good. Maybe you can fill in some of the extremely wide gaps?"

"Ethan!" Tom tried to stand before Ed forced him back onto the couch.

"We gathered that something happened to him. You kept saying 'they' took him. Who, Tom?"

Tom rubbed at his temples, willing the headache to subside. He wondered briefly if he'd ever feel normal again. "Two men… convicts who escaped from a prison bus that crashed. They ambushed us, shot me, and took the horses. And they took Ethan."

The creases on Ed's face deepened. "Why in the world would they take the boy?"

"They were still cuffed," Tom explained. He stared at the candle on the table behind Ed, recalling the scene. "They didn't know anything about horses except that they wanted them. Maybe they figured Ethan could help…and would be easy to control. I don't know, but I'm afraid once they manage to remove their chains and learn how to ride, he won't be needed any longer."

"Maybe they'll just let him go," Ed offered.

Tom shook his head, and then winced at the pain the motion caused him. "No. They're killers, Ed."

"How do you know that?"

Tom looked down at his hands and then cleared his throat. "I've been tracking them. Fairly easy to do, considering the terrain. They've already killed a man." Tom looked up at Ed and swallowed hard. "Some farmer, not far from here. He confronted the three of them yesterday morning, when he heard them out by his barn. I got there pretty late last night, but from what I could tell, I think they're still trying to cut the chains on their handcuffs. They shot him dead in front of his family, Ed."

Tom wished his memory of the woman sobbing over her husband's death was as fuzzy as the time he'd spent on the bike. His resolve hardened, and he focused on Ed's face. "I have to find Ethan."

"You will." Ed pointed at the fresh bandages on Tom's arm. "Looks like you caught a bit of luck with that one. Could have been a lot worse. Although I gotta say, you did a shockingly poor job bandaging it."

Moving his right arm to test its strength, Tom was relieved to discover it was a lot better off than his head. Looking at a glass of water and plate of half-eaten scrambled eggs on the table next to Ed, he was glad he'd managed to find his way back to their house. However, as his thoughts continued to sharpen, he felt an overwhelming urge to get moving again. He was already a day behind Ethan and he couldn't afford to lose more time.

Ed must have picked up on his restlessness, because he slapped his knees and then stood, offering Tom a hand. "Let's get you back on your feet."

As the older man helped pull him to his feet, Tom heard Marnie gagging in another room. It was followed by the unmistakable sound of vomiting. He looked at Ed questioningly. "Is Marnie okay?" When the older man didn't answer, Tom took a closer look at his friend. He'd been so consumed with his own situation that he'd missed some obvious signs. Even in the poor lighting Tom could see that Ed was obviously pale and his clothes looked baggy.

"I want you to take our two horses." Ed moved to the kitchen and poured some water from a large plastic container into a cup. As he walked past Tom on his way to the back bedroom, he paused. "I've put some things in your backpack I thought you might find useful."

Tom was deeply troubled by the finality of his dismissal. "Is it radiation sickness?"

"Probably." Ed flinched when Marnie began vomiting again. "Nausea medication helped the first day, after you'd been here, but not anymore. She can't keep anything down...or in."

Tom and Ethan were both suffering from such mild symptoms that he hadn't thought it was a serious risk. It had only been three days, so it was shocking how quickly she'd deteriorated. "We'll bring the horses back." He didn't know what else to say.

Ed shook his head. "No." He turned then and looked at Tom. "Marnie isn't going to make it much longer. Maybe it's because of her age, or because she has an autoimmune condition, but she's much worse off than I am."

Tom felt even more helpless than before. "I can stay for a while and help you," he offered. "Maybe there's something else we can do for her."

Ed reached out and clasped onto Tom's good arm. "Marnie and I have both led good, full lives, Tom. I appreciate the offer, but there's nothing for you to do."

Tom placed his hand over Ed's, still on his arm, and squeezed it. "I'll never forget you and Marnie, or your kindness."

Clearing his throat, Ed straightened and took a step back, his mouth forming a hard, determined line. "Now. You go saddle the two mares and go find your son. I pray that you'll somehow be led to him."

"I know where he's going."

Ed tilted his head questioningly at Tom. "How's that?"

Tom reached into his jeans pocket and pulled out an old, crumpled hardware store receipt. Holding it up, he turned it over to reveal a hand-written message on the back of it. *Dad—we're going to Virginia, Idaho. Ethan.* "The woman found this sticking out of her husband's shirt pocket. She—" his voice cracked and he coughed once. "She gave it to me when I explained what had happened."

"He's a smart boy," Ed reassured him. "He'll be okay."

Tom forced himself to walk to the front door, overwhelmed with both leaving the couple, and the prospect of trying to find Ethan. The farmer's wife told him that Virginia was a pretty small place, but there was no guarantee they'd actually be there. Or, they could have come and gone by the time he reached it. They could be anywhere by then and as they got closer to some bigger cities, his odds of coming across someone who could confirm a sighting was becoming slimmer.

With the horses, he had a much better chance of catching them. He'd ride hard for the town of Virginia and, if he was lucky, the storm he saw brewing in the south wouldn't head their way. If it rained, he'd lose the ability to track the other horses.

As he opened the door and stepped through into the new day, Ed gave him one final directive. "You find your boy, Tom, and get him home. You get him back to Mercy."

CHAPTER 11

THAN
Pocatello, Idaho

ONE OF THE police cruiser's tires exploded with a surprisingly loud whooshing sound, causing Ethan to fall away from the scene and duck for cover. "Oomph," he grunted as he hit the ground next to a wall of the parking structure. Pieces of smoldering rubber splattered on the cement by his hands and he brushed frantically at his back when he felt something hit it.

Billy laughed as he lifted Ethan by the scruff of his neck and shoved him toward the vehicle. "It's just the tires. Cars rarely explode like in the movies. A total sham."

It was still early enough in the morning that the car fire provided the brightest source of light to see by. Not that Ethan necessarily wanted to see anything out on the streets. He suddenly longed to go back inside the parking garage, even though only moments before he wanted nothing more than to leave its confining space.

They'd been forced inside the day before, after their plight through Pocatello had proven too dangerous, even for the armed convicts. The only good thing was that they'd lost at least half a day because of it. The bad part was that while the chaos of the city offered Ethan some opportunities to escape, the agonizing reality was that at the moment, he was safer with Decker and Billy.

Billy kicked at an unmoving body next to the car. As Ethan neared, he saw that the man was wearing a police uniform, but was stripped of all his gear. He was also beaten to death.

"Good riddance." Billy spat at the ground next to the cop and the curl to his lip enhanced his ugliness. He was a wiry, medium-sized man in his thirties, but his long greasy hair and bad teeth made him look older. "Where were you yesterday when we could have used ya?" Billy jeered, holding up the hands that he'd finally managed to free the day before.

Ethan looked at Billy with a new level of contempt and spoke before he could check himself. "Are you really stupid enough to think his keys would have worked on those prison cuffs?"

Billy considered the comment for a moment while laughing, then pivoted toward Ethan and backhanded him. Hard.

Staggering under the impact, Ethan vaguely wondered what he looked like now that he'd become a punching bag over the past few days. He resisted raising a hand to touch the new bruise on his right cheek. It was a small act of defiance but he took what he could get.

"If you're done smacking your kid around, you can give us your bag." A man in his early twenties stepped out from the other side of the burning car. He was holding a crowbar that he pointed at Billy for emphasis. "Then, you can show us where you put your horses. We've been waiting for you."

Ethan forgot about his stinging face and saw that there were four more men and a woman gathered behind the one with the crowbar. They were all filthy, their clothes torn, singed, and covered in both dirt and blood. One man held a large knife, another what looked like part of an iron fence. The woman clutched a bat, her eyes wild and her face so distorted with feral rage that Ethan couldn't guess her age. He took it all in, and was reminded of a scene from a horrible knock-off of *Blade Runner.* That he was so close to laughing about it scared him. It wasn't funny. Nothing about what he'd seen in the city over the past day was funny.

The horses were the main reason they'd been forced to hide. While there were others on horseback in the city, they were a growing commodity and people were already willing to kill for a Snickers bar, let alone transportation.

Six days since the flash. Ethan had no way of knowing how the majority of the bodies in the streets got there, although some were obviously from violence. The others? He figured they died from either dehydration from lack of water, or other illnesses due to the conditions. Fires were still burning, and even the smoke that settled among the buildings couldn't camouflage the stench of death mingled with raw sewage and garbage.

Thanks to his fascination with survival stories, Ethan knew that without fluids, you could die in as little as three days, especially with the heat they'd been having. From what they'd heard, looting broke out the first night and then once it became clear help wasn't moving in or the power being restored, survivors turned to pillaging and fleeing with as much as they could carry.

As they'd approached the city early the previous day, they encountered dozens of people wandering aimlessly on the interstate. Some cautioned them to go around Pocatello, that it wasn't safe, but most were beyond the ability to speak or to care about anyone else. There were random camps and some groups staked out to the west of the interstate, where there was a small river, but it seemed that most of the people capable of surviving had moved on during the first few days following the event. All that was left at that point were the dying and those who preyed on the dying.

Billy slowly unclipped the chest strap on his backpack and then started to shrug his left arm out. As the pack was falling, he used his right hand to pull the gun from his waistband and bring it around. A look of shock wasn't even fully registered on their assailant's face before it was obliterated by a bullet. The sharp report echoed off the concrete buildings around them as the body crumpled to the ground and Billy pointed the gun at the next man closest to them.

Bullets were another commodity and the only reason they'd made it that far without losing their horses and gear. While Decker managed to find the auto shop and equipment necessary to remove the cuffs that had driven him into the city against all reason, ammunition had disappeared as fast as water. Those who were armed in the beginning had already used up their bullets, reducing the majority of the weapons to nothing more than blunt objects.

"Stop!" the man pled. He dropped his iron rod and took a step back. "We'll just—"

Another shot exploded in unison with a blossom of dark crimson on the man's chest. He was wearing a white T-shirt and he stumbled backwards and looked down at the spreading stain with as much shock as Ethan felt. He fell to his knees.

Billy swung the gun to the next person but the rest of them were already running. "That's right!" he yelled, his voice cracking. "You just keep running!"

Ethan stared at the gun, but not out of fear. If he was right, Billy had just used the last bullet.

"What's going on out here?" Decker came running from the entrance at their backs. "I sent you to check on things, not announce our position to the whole freaking city."

Billy turned away from the fresh carnage he'd added to the macabre mosaic. "Hey, uh...Decker. Man, I think it's clear now." Billy fidgeted with the handle of the gun, likely hoping Decker hadn't counted the shots. Ethan was amazed the moron hadn't shot himself. If he could only get so lucky.

The sun was beginning to shine in between the buildings and the second man fell over into a patch of light. Decker stared at him first, then made a disgusted sound when he saw the face of the original attacker.

"They knew we had the horses," Billy attempted to explain. "Said they were waitin' for us, Decker."

Ethan eyed the door and took a couple of steps in its direction. The horses were up on the level above them. Could he make it to them in time to get away while the two men were busy arguing?

Decker turned then and stared at Ethan while gesturing to Billy. "Come on. Let's go now before everyone's awake. We should make it to Charlie's place by tonight. It's just south of Virginia, about forty miles from here according to the map."

His fleeting chance at escape gone, Ethan did as he was told and followed the convicts into the dark recesses of the garage. As he walked, Ethan worked on another plan. Now that they were free of the cuffs and almost to their destination, he wasn't sure why they were even keeping him with them...or alive. He needed to get away.

Decker had been riding Tango, forcing Ethan onto the third mare and the only horse without a saddle. He could still easily outride both of the convicts and now that he *thought* they were out of bullets, it might be worth taking the chance. It meant leaving Tango behind, which was another reason he'd hesitated before. Ideally, Ethan had hoped to catch Billy falling asleep while on watch over the past three nights, and then make off with the horses. However, unlike the movies, nothing was playing out the way he'd imagined it. Billy proved to be good at staying up all night, while Ethan ended up falling asleep, exhausted from the constant stress and pain. He'd come to understand why they continued to hit him the way they did. It was never enough to incapacitate him, but it wore him down and made him cower from the next expected blow, no matter how hard he tried to resist it.

"What are you waiting for?" Decker barked.

Ethan jumped. Billy and Decker were already on their horses, staring at him. Half-expecting to get a bullet in him, if there were any left, Ethan scurried in the semi-darkness of the open parking area, collecting their gear. Thanks to his newly discovered talent for pillaging vacant houses, they'd acquired a decent-sized hoard of useful things during their trek south. Silently, he tied it all down on his horse before hauling himself up onto her back.

As they made their way down the exit ramp from the garage and out onto the street, Ethan took his expected spot, in between the two convicts. They both had their guns drawn and made a point of showing them to anyone that was out in the open. Ethan did his best to ignore the burning car they passed, with both the old and fresh corpses near it. The sounds of sobbing and cries for help echoed around the concrete buildings, mixing together. It was underscored by moans that escalated to screams, and Ethan chose not to think what was causing it. Random gunfire still rang out sporadically in the distance, urging them to move forward as quickly as possible. It was a world gone mad.

They only had a few blocks to go before reaching an onramp to Interstate 15 and Ethan breathed a sigh of relief when they reached it. He'd been taking shallow breaths the whole way to avoid gagging on the disgusting odors so he was feeling light headed. Decker was likely doing the same, because he kicked at Tango until the horse broke into a gallop down the blacktop. Ethan and Billy followed, leaving the city behind them.

Ethan took a moment to appreciate the feeling of freedom the movement gave him, and the fresher air they were running toward. As he watched Decker handle Tango, the brief respite from his anxiety came to a quick end. The men had learned enough in the past three days about horses and how to ride to make do without his help. Ethan knew he was out of time. Once they reached this Charlie guy's place, he was as good as dead.

CHAPTER 12

S TEVIE
Northwestern Washington State

"COME ON, SLAYER!" Stevie patted his thigh and then rolled his eyes when the black lab sat staring solemnly at him. The blue tag on his collar read "Snoopy", but Stevie thought it was a dumb name and had been trying to change it to something similar…just much, much cooler. "Fine. Snoopy. Come here, Snoopy!" Snoopy barked once and then leaped forward, running past the boy and into the field beyond.

Twelve-year-old Steven Estop broke out into rare laughter at the young dog's antics as he rolled in the tall grass. He'd rescued the dog two days before, and now he honestly couldn't imagine life without him anymore. Stevie frowned at the memory. He didn't like to think about "those" days. The darkest ones after "it" happened.

Stevie turned and looked back at his small, postcard-perfect house. It sat on three acres at the end of a dirt road. His mom worked hard to be able to afford it, which was why he'd been home alone six days ago. Stevie had talked his mom into letting him stay home by himself that summer while she worked. His birthday was in September so he was practically a teenager, and he sure didn't need a sitter. His stomach cramped at the thought and his breathing quickened.

"She'll be home soon. She'll be home soon," Stevie hummed the words so that it sounded like he was singing a song. It had become his mantra. He'd learned that word recently while watching a movie at his friend Jay's and it seemed right. It was an R-rated movie, one his mom would have never let him watch, but Jay had Wi-Fi and a laptop.

Snoopy barked again and pulled Stevie out of his daze, which was something that was happening more lately. He didn't know if it was because he wasn't eating enough, or maybe he was just losing it. Probably both.

He wondered what Jay was doing. If he was alone, too. Probably not. Jay's parents were still married, his mom didn't work, and he had an older sister. Stevie had started to ride his bike to his friend's house twice already, finding the farther he got away from his house, the greater his anxiety grew until he couldn't breathe anymore and had to turn back. It was too far.

The two of them had moved to the little house out in the country the summer before. It was over a half-hour drive into town and nearly an hour to his mom's job where she worked as a nurse. She claimed it was worth it. While it wasn't a working farm, there was lots of space and not many neighbors. His mom said she felt safe there and that eventually, they would get chickens and a horse and he'd grow to love it.

She'd been right, and Stevie had grown to love the trails and crisp air and all the places he could ride his bike. At night, he could climb out his second-story bedroom window and lie on the porch roof to watch the stars. He'd done that the night before, only the northern lights were so bright he could hardly see the Milky Way.

Stevie frowned at the overgrown yard. The grass needed to be mowed, but nothing worked and he didn't know what to do. His eyes suddenly filled with tears and he struggled with the unreasonable, overwhelming guilt he felt about letting the yard look bad. His mom would be disappointed when she came home and saw it.

Snoopy barked again.

Stevie sniffed and wiped at his cheek. It probably left a dirt streak, but that didn't matter. Although he had changed his clothes a couple of times, there wasn't any way to wash them, leaving him as dirty as the last time he went camping with Jay and his family. Stevie was afraid to waste any of the drinking water to even clean his face. Maybe he'd bike down to the creek that afternoon and go swimming with his clothes on.

Stevie knew not to drink the water from the creek. Not without boiling it first. His mom had told him that a bunch of times after they first moved in, and then Mr. and Mrs. Shipley said the same thing when he saw them the second day after "it". They were gone now.

Stevie didn't realize he'd started walking again and he looked up at the Shipleys' house in surprise. He'd made it all the way to the other end of their street, to his second-nearest neighbor. Snoopy was waiting for him on the front porch, sitting patiently by the door.

"Good boy," Stevie told the dog as he opened the unlocked entrance.

The first day, after "it" happened, Stevie had gone across the street to their closest neighbor. A man named Hector lived there but was always working and kept to himself. He was gone that day and hadn't come back.

Stevie had gone back home then and decided to just wait for

his mom to get home. He had no way of knowing then that anything more than the power had gone out. He didn't have a cellphone and he thought the house phone didn't work because of the outage. Their electricity went out a couple times the previous year due to weather and it wasn't a big deal. The light was a big deal, though, and it scared him. When his mom didn't come home from work that night, he *knew* something really, really bad had happened.

The next day, he went to the Shipleys' and they'd fed him and let him stay there until it got dark. They were nice and wanted him to spend the night but he'd refused. He was convinced his mom would come home. He'd sat in the window of their front room the whole time watching for her. When it got dark so he couldn't see anymore, he insisted on going home. What if she got there, couldn't find him, and left?

Stevie entered the Shipleys' kitchen now and wrinkled his nose. Even with the fridge closed, the smell of rotting food still filled the room. He quickly made his way into the walk-in pantry and began filling his backpack. He wasn't stealing. After he refused to leave with the Shipleys to go to their kid's farm a few days away, they said he could have whatever he wanted.

After his pack was stuffed with Pop-Tarts, crackers, peanut butter, and chips, he went into the attached garage, where half a case of bottled water remained. He stood looking at it for a moment. While Steven may have been considered a child still by most adults, he was intelligent. He could easily estimate he had about five days of drinking water left. He'd need to start going through more houses soon.

The thought made Stevie's stomach hurt again and he could hear his rapid breathing echoing off the cement floor. He tried to swallow, but his mouth was too dry. He didn't like to think about going into other people's houses. Bad things were waiting there.

The first time he tried was four days after "it". He figured

Hector wasn't coming back, so what would he care if Stevie took a look around inside? The front door was locked, but the back slider wasn't. As soon as he'd pushed it open, the stench hit him. Gagging, he'd looked down in horror at a dead cat, its eyes writhing with maggots. It must have died trying to get out through the glass door. Stevie didn't know Hector even had a cat. He'd never seen one outside.

He'd run home when, after only a few minutes, feelings of guilt prompted him to get on his bike and begin a door-to-door search he'd named "Operation Rescue". In the end, he only managed to reach ten houses after riding around all afternoon. Three of them were occupied, counting the Shipleys. In the vacant houses he did manage to rescue one other cat, and Snoopy. The last house... It was so much worse than Hector's, and was the reason why Stevie never went beyond those ten.

He didn't know who she was and it was hard to tell how old the woman had been when she died. Her front door had been unlocked and Stevie found her in the recliner, probably watching an afternoon soap when "it" happened. The Shipleys told him about how there was some sort of magnetic pulse thingy that made everything stop. *Everything.* When he told them about...her, they said she might have had something in her body that stopped working, like a pacemaker. Stevie's grandma had one of those and he tried not to think about what that meant.

Snoopy sat at his feet and whined. Stevie reached out and absently pet the lab's head. "Oh!" he gasped, looking down then at the dog. "Sorry, buddy. I didn't forget. Promise." Crossing over to a shelf on the other side of the garage, he took down a box of Milk-Bones. The Shipleys had a dog, too, but couldn't carry all the dog stuff they had when they left. He tossed a bone to Snoopy and smiled as he watched the dog gobble it up like it was a totally normal day in a normal world.

A cloud moved over the sun outside, plunging the garage into a murky grayness as it only had one window. Spurred into motion, Stevie clutched the dog treats to his chest and rushed over to the water. Grabbing six bottles, he crammed them into the remaining pockets of his pack and then grunted with the effort of putting it on his back.

He didn't like the dark.

His heart beat a quick cadence until he was outside, where he took several gulping breaths to calm it. Snoopy danced in a circle around him and Stevie tried to focus on the animal. It helped to block out everything else. The fact that he was mostly alone. That he was going to have to figure out how to use the barbeque to boil water soon, and remember how to tie a hook on to his pole. There were some fish in the creek and he was determined to catch one.

His mom would be so proud of him when she came home and saw him *cooking* fish for dinner. Stevie's breathing slowed then and he thought about how she would hug him and tell him everything was going to be okay. He started back for his house, a boy with his dog just strolling through the tall grass, humming a song.

"She'll be home soon. She'll be home soon…soon, soon, soon."

CHAPTER 13

HLOE
Mercy, Montana

CHLOE SAT on the edge of the bed in Sandy Miller's guestroom and stared at her hands for so long that her eyes stung when she finally blinked. "So much for sleeping all day," she muttered. After a restless night of odd dreams, she'd finally dozed off, only to be awakened by Crissy kicking her in the back. Chloe glanced over at her friend, who was still sound asleep, and was thankful that at least one of them was getting a reprieve from their waking nightmare.

She was still struggling to come to terms with what Mrs. Miller had told them the night before. It was so much worse than any of them had fathomed. Now what? What were they going to do?

A soft knock at the door made Chloe jump, and she looked up to see their host poking her head in. "Did I wake you?"

Chloe shook her head and then stood slowly so she wouldn't

disturb Crissy. There was plenty of sunlight coming in through the one large window in the room, so she might as well get up. Padding to the door in bare feet, she gratefully accepted a robe the older woman held out to her. She'd been reduced to wearing her one remaining T-shirt that wasn't filthy as a nightgown. "Thank you, Mrs. Miller."

"Ugh. I'm not that old yet. Please, call me Sandy."

Chloe smiled up at Sandy. She was a tall woman with broad shoulders and sparkling blue eyes. She reminded Chloe of her grandma, who'd passed away two years ago. She'd always told Chloe she got her spunk from her, and something told her Sandy wasn't short on spirit.

"How's Trevor?" Chloe asked as she followed Sandy through the large house and out onto the back patio. She had to admit that in an odd way, she was troubled to not hear the younger boy's ragged breathing all night long. She'd grown accustomed to it.

As soon as they stepped outside, Chloe smelled a medley of cooked eggs and onions. Searching out the source, she saw an outside cooking area off to one side. Red bricks had been used to create a stove, with stone counters extending to each side and bar stool seating. Unique wooden chairs were clustered around a picnic table in the center of the patio, offering more seating. The barbeque had been jury-rigged so that a cast-iron skillet was set over a smoldering fire. Sandy removed the food and scooped some out onto a nearby plate before offering it to Chloe. Thick slices of fried potatoes were mixed in with the eggs, onions, and even mushrooms.

"This looks amazing." Chloe's mouth was watering so much that she had to wipe at it. It tasted even better than it looked.

Sandy laughed. "Trevor is doing fine. He and Ripley already ate and headed into town to see the doctor."

"He's okay?" Chloe's brows drew together with concern.

"Oh, yes. I just thought it would be a good idea to have her look him over, considering how much epinephrine he's been injected with over the past couple of days." Sandy led them to an arrangement of outdoor furniture and they sat down opposite each other. "He claims to be breathing better, though."

Chloe shoveled the last bite of food into her mouth and washed it down with a glass of water that was already sitting on the table near her. She closed her eyes and relished the cool, crisp water. She'd gotten used to the hot, plastic-tasting water from her camel pack. "Where did this come from?" she asked, holding the glass up.

Sandy stood and motioned for Chloe to follow her. The pride she felt for the Miller farm was evident as she pointed out the different features. "Over there's the primary barn; the stockyard is behind it. We have five hundred acres that go up and over the mountain, which includes two lakes and some of the world's best pasture." They stepped through a gate and out of a tall wire fence surrounding the backyard area. "This is to keep the elk and deer out," she explained. "Otherwise, it would be impossible to have a garden."

Chloe looked back at the far corner of the large yard and saw a good thirty-by-thirty section cordoned off with a two-foot high fence to keep rabbits out. Two rows of corn dominated the back part of it, while other things she wasn't familiar with filled the rest. Fresh dirt was turned over outside of the fence.

"I'm working on expanding it," Sandy said. "It's late to be planting anything, but with everything that's happened, I figured I should try."

"The food I just ate," Chloe said, looking at Sandy with a new level of respect. "Did all of that come from here?"

Sandy laughed and began walking again, shooing at a chicken along the way. "Of course it did, Chloe. This is a working farm. While it hasn't been self-sustaining for a very long time, it once was, back when my grandfather first built it." She stopped in front of what looked like a cast-iron candy cane.

Chloe studied the apparatus, taking in the moving lever and faucet-shaped head. "Wait, is that some sort of water pump?"

Sandy smiled and nodded approvingly. "Yes! Very good. That's exactly what it is. A deep well hand pump, which used to be the only source of drinkable water on the farm. My father installed an indoor one at one point, in the kitchen, but my husband, in all of his misplaced wisdom, removed it twenty years ago."

"This is the water I was drinking?"

"Some of the best water in the valley," Sandy said with pride. "Go on. Try it."

Chloe lifted the handle and with some effort, was able to compress it once and then twice, the motion becoming easier with each pump. Soon, cold water was flowing and she stopped, feeling guilty about wasting it.

"There's more water in there than we've ever been able to use," Sandy said. "Though not every well is created equal, and plenty of folks around here have struggled with a lower water table the past few years. And that isn't to say I'm not struggling now with the cattle."

Chloe looked at her questioningly. "How so?"

"Well, both the water used for watering the fields as well as the cattle troughs is normally pumped from this well." Sandy pointed to a small wooden structure located twenty feet away. "The *electric* pump is housed there, as well as all the piping for the main house and the barns. Without it, I can manage to carry in enough drinking water, but the cattle and fields are a completely different story."

"You said there's a couple of lakes on the property," Chloe replied. "Can't the cows drink that?"

Sandy smiled again at Chloe's quick rationalizing. "That's

exactly what they're doing. Well, from the creek that leads out of the largest one, to be exact. The problem is distance and location. I can get away with leaving them in the upper pasture for now, except I'll eventually have to bring them down when the weather turns, and I'll need to have solved my water supply problem by then. Especially since the grass they normally live off the rest of the year is going to burn up over the next few months without watering."

Sandy started back to the house, but Chloe stayed for a minute and looked up at the land rising steeply behind them, up the side of the mountain. She then turned to study the lower fields and stockyard, and then finally the pump.

"Let's go find you some clothes," Sandy called back to her. "I think some of my grandson's T-shirts and sweats he left here last year might work."

Chloe rushed to catch up, ignoring the fact that Sandy wanted to dress her in some boy's old clothes. "What about a gravity-fed water system?"

Sandy paused just inside the large sliding-glass doors. Turning around to face Chloe, she crossed her arms over her chest and tilted her head at her. "What do you mean?"

Chloe moved past her and sat on a tall barstool at the kitchen counter. "You said the lake was in the upper pastures. So, do it how they used to in the...ugh, I dunno how long ago it was, but hasn't pretty much every ancient civilization used some sort of gravity-driven system to move water and waste around?"

Sandy sat on the stool next to Chloe, squinting as she stared off into space, thinking. "Instead of moving the herd to the source, move the source to the herd," she mumbled. "It would take a ton of piping." She grabbed at a notebook and pen on the counter and began drawing a picture. "But if I moved the trough here...and created some sort of cistern here..." She looked up from her rough doodles and stared at Chloe. "Why in the world didn't I think of this?"

"Probably because you were too close to the problem to see it clearly," Chloe offered. "That's what my dad would always—" she trailed off, her voice catching. Guilt once again took her breath away and her thoughts became jumbled. Where were her parents? Were they even alive? Those questions had been a big part of keeping her awake most of the night. The not knowing was incredibly frustrating and she felt so helpless.

Sandy placed a hand on Chloe's shoulder. She was thankful that the older woman didn't try to hug her. She didn't need a shoulder to cry on, just some reassurance. "I'm sorry, Chloe. I know this has all been a horrible shock. Didn't you say last night that you're from Washington State? From what we've heard, that's likely one of the safer places to be right now. You have to believe that you'll be reunited with them again at some point. Right now, though, they would want you to do whatever was necessary to stay safe and trying to travel that far would *not* be safe. Not yet."

Chloe swallowed and then cleared her throat before meeting Sandy's empathetic eyes. Again, she was reminded of Grandma Benson and could almost imagine the floral perfume she always wore. "What am I supposed to do?" Her voice came out thin and broken, mirroring how she felt inside.

"I have plenty of room here on the farm," Sandy said with firm resolution. "And plenty of work that needs to be done." She stood then and went to one of the bookshelves next to the fireplace. From it, she lifted a framed picture and brought it back to where Chloe sat. "This is my son, Thomas, and my grandson, Ethan."

Chloe took the picture, her eyes welling with tears as she understood the depth of Sandy's pain. "Where are they?" she whispered.

Sandy's nostrils flared and her jaw clenched. "They're on their way home." When Chloe remained silent, she took the picture back and held it tightly to her chest. "Thomas went down to Vegas to bring Ethan back for the summer. They stopped along the way to pick up some horses. I received a text message a few hours before…the flashpoint. I figure they were around three to five hundred miles away."

Chloe hung her head and thought about the various scenarios that could have occurred. "He must be pretty tough if you're his mom," she finally offered, grinning up at Sandy.

Laughing, the older woman sniffed once and then went to put the picture back. "Young lady, you have no idea."

Bishop tromped up onto the back porch then, dusting his pants off before coming inside. He was wearing leather work gloves and there was a thick sheen of sweat on his forehead. "I split that wood, Sandy, and stacked it up alongside the garage. If you tell me where your tools are, I'll go fix the door on the henhouse. You don't want them left exposed at night."

"Thank you, Bishop," Sandy offered. "There are some pesky coyotes hanging around lately, so you're right about that door. I've been meaning to fix it, but there's simply too many things for me to do."

Chloe was strangely relieved that Sandy wasn't using Bishop's real name. Perhaps because it was a simple constant in a sea of changing tides.

A knock at the front door ended any further conversation. Chloe figured it would be Ripley and Trevor returning, and was surprised to see a man in a police uniform at the door, instead.

"Deputy Campbell," Sandy announced, swinging the door wide so the man could come inside. "It's nice to see you. Is everything okay? Patty…I mean, Mayor Woods asked for an updated food list by tomorrow."

The deputy removed his hat and nodded at Sandy, but then

paused when he saw Chloe and Bishop. "I heard you had some visitors," he said while gesturing at them with his hat. Looking back at the ranch owner, he was clearly uncomfortable. "Um, Mrs. Miller, the mayor has called another meeting for this afternoon that she wants you to attend." He glanced at Bishop. "As well as your guests."

Sandy tilted her head at him and crossed her arms. "Now, Jim, are you going to tell me what this is about? You're looking like the boy I caught swimming in my lake when he was what, about fifteen?"

Jim shuffled his feet and fiddled with the brim of his hat. "I'm sorry, Mrs. Miller, there's been some new discussions about... outsiders. Your friends who went into town will meet you there," he said to Bishop. "You'd best bring their things."

"What do you mean by that?" Sandy pressed, her patience clearly wearing thin.

"We're closing off the town to any newcomers," the deputy announced, slamming the hat back onto his head. Chloe's new sense of belonging rapidly faded as he stared first at her and then Bishop. "I'm afraid you're going to have to leave Mercy."

CHAPTER 14

PATTY
Mercy City Hall

PATTY DID her best to avoid eye contact with the group of strangers with Sandy. The three kids and young woman were seated in chairs against the wall, but the man was standing with a stern look on his handsome face. She guessed he wasn't more than a few years younger than Sandy, maybe fifty, and was very fit for his age. Based on what she'd heard, she had expected a more needy-looking group of destitute hikers. It was going to make a difficult situation even more impossible.

Gary leaned over from where he was sitting beside Patty and spoke under his breath. "Is it really necessary to have them here?" He glanced up at the group of strangers and then back at Patty. "I thought they would already be gone by now."

Patty bit back the retort that instantly came to mind. While she and Gary had been working surprisingly well together, they still had their fundamental differences. "I asked that they attend. We at least owe them and Sandy an explanation."

"To what purpose?" he pressed. "We don't owe them a thing. You heard what Sheriff Waters said."

"Perhaps the sheriff can share his update with all of us," Ned Allen interrupted. Gary had the decency to at least look chagrined at the previous mayor's obvious admonishment of their not-so-private conversation.

"Of course," Patty agreed, standing to face the large group. The meeting room in city hall was nearly overflowing with the combination of council members, committee heads, and other town leaders. She took a couple of steps back to where the white-board sat and turning, solemnly wiped the number 652 off with her fist. The marker squeaked as she wrote out 648, the sound eerily loud in a room that had fallen silent.

"Dr. Olsen informed me this morning that we've lost three more residents in the past day. Two of them from dehydration or other complications brought on by what is believed to be radiation poisoning." Patty raised her hands as the room grew loud with multiple questions being asked at once.

"I believe it was partly due to underlying conditions," Melissa shouted. Patty gestured to the doctor, so she stood and joined the mayor at the front of the room. "It would seem that most of us have suffered only mild headaches and some nausea. The very young and old tolerated this less and, in some cases, needed varying degrees of intervention, and are now quickly recovering. The deaths were among those already compromised, such as being diabetic, battling kidney failure, and in one case ongoing chemotherapy treatment for lung cancer. I'm not saying it makes any of those deaths less traumatic, I just want to urge you all not to panic. There was a very definitive wave in the onset and peak of symptoms, which I think we are past."

Sheriff Waters stood as Dr. Olsen took her seat. "I'm sorry to inform you all that the fourth death was Kyle Tucker." A fresh wave of questions and side conversations created a loud droning and the sheriff clapped his hands to restore some order. "His brother Aaron returned very early this morning. As you know, they both volunteered to ride to Helena as scouts and report back on what's happening outside of Mercy. They successfully reached their relative's property near the city, but were attacked on their way back."

"Attacked?" Mr. Sullivan asked. Although most of his store's goods had already been dispersed, he retained a place in what was becoming known as the town's new government. A group of respected leaders all given a voice in the choices being made that would determine everyone's fate in the coming days.

"Kyle was shot," the sheriff explained. "For his horse. At least, that was the attempt which didn't succeed. He was able to get a shot off before he was hit, and Aaron killed one of the others, prompting the rest of them to run away. The two of them made it back to their uncle's place, where Kyle ended up bleeding to death."

"People are just running around shooting each other?" Gary asked, his face ashen. "My God, how could things break down this fast?"

"That wasn't even inside the city," Sheriff Waters countered. "According to Aaron, they didn't even attempt going into Helena. He said it looked like most of the city center had either burned or was still burning and the fire had spread to a large portion of the town. It was total chaos with looting, fights, and no sign of any government or law. It's been two days more since then, so people are going to be even more desperate to meet their basic needs. They'll be turning from fear to a blind panic for survival. It won't be someone willing to kill for a horse, it'll be a feral attack for water or food."

"And you want to send these kids out into that?" Sandy stood and pointed an accusatory finger at her best friend. "How can you be so callous?"

Patty cringed. She had planned on speaking with Sandy prior to the meeting, to explain things, but had been delayed at the gas station. Al was already running low on gas and the generators would be dry in less than a week. She glanced at one of the precious lights, resigned to the fact that they'd be unplugging it after the meeting. They had to conserve as much as they could for the clinic.

"It isn't that we don't feel for them." Patty couldn't look Sandy in the eyes. She knew there was no way she could justify the move to her. "But Aaron made it clear that there's a mass exodus underway at Helena, and while most of them are going in other directions, it's inevitable that some will make their way here. It's simple math, Sandy. We don't have enough resources to take in outsiders."

"I'm not staying."

Patty looked at the woman referred to as Ripley. She'd seen her earlier at the clinic with the boy who had asthma issues. Melissa had given him an inhaler, another poignant example of why closing the city down was imperative. Patty couldn't help but think that they now had one less inhaler for their own people and it was a life-saving medication.

"I don't care how dangerous you say it is," Ripley said to the sheriff. "My fiancé is in Helena, and I'm going."

The short girl with spikey black hair with purple tips reached out then and took Ripley's hand. Patty thought her name was Chloe. Ripley looked surprised by the gesture and gave Chloe's hand a squeeze before turning back to the sheriff.

"Aaron is going back to his uncle's place tomorrow," Sheriff Waters said to her, giving a small nod. "You can ride with him."

"His uncle has agreed to let us use their property as an express station," Caleb explained to the room. "In spite of what's occurred, we're going ahead with the plan. We'll of course send several armed men with Aaron and the extra horses. We hope to establish a solid line of communication and supplies, and possibly expand our reach eventually."

"The Pony Express?" Bishop asked.

Caleb smiled at him. "Why reinvent the wheel? It worked quite well in the past."

Bishop smiled back in agreement. "I understand your position," he then said, turning to Patty. "You have to do what's best for your people. We're a drain on supplies and have brought nothing to the table in return. I'm from Butte and my only family —my son—is stationed in Germany, so I really don't have a reason to try and risk getting back home. I can take the kids to our Trek Thru Trouble office. We'll figure something out from there."

"That's a week's walk from here!" Sandy countered. "Anything of value or use that *was* there is likely already taken by now."

"I don't mean to marginalize your situation," Fire Chief Martinez said, clearing his throat. "But we have some more pressing issues that also need to be discussed. How are we coming on the water?" He directed his question to Patty and she tried not to let the anxiety show on her face. "I know a lot of folks have been working hard to get it moved around to those who need it, and I'm afraid we aren't going to be able to keep up for long."

Patty sat back down next to Caleb and was incredibly thankful for the hand he rested on her arm. That simple touch, his show of support, lent her the strength she was lacking on her own. "Caleb has been working with Ned and Al to come up with a way to move the water more efficiently from the spring."

"There's no easy or quick solution," Caleb interjected. "Not without electricity. We don't have a strong enough working generator, or enough fuel, to get the city's water system running again. That leaves us with physically moving it and creating an effective system, and that will take time."

"I was the city engineer for Butte," the man beside Sandy interjected softly while looking up from his hands.

Patty tilted her head at Bishop. "You're a civil engineer?"

Bishop nodded. "I've worked on developing roads, bridges, dams, and water supplies. Pretty much any element that's part of a city's infrastructure. I'd be happy to go over some plans with you, Caleb, on what might work best for your situation based on where this spring is located."

Caleb leaned in close to Patty. "I could really use his expertise."

"I also need their help," Sandy said loudly, still standing. She walked up to the table opposite Patty and looked pleadingly at her friend. "With Tom gone, I'm struggling. There's too much for me to do on my own without the help of any farm equipment or running water. You put me in charge of organizing food distribution for a reason, Patty, and I'm telling you right now that I can't do it without some help. If you want me to share my cattle, hens, and water with my neighbors, then I need ranch hands." She looked around the room at the rest of the attendees. "Unless some you want to abandon your own places to come help me, then I'd say we've already been presented with the perfect solution." Sandy gestured to the strangers behind her. "You might think it's easier to just label all outsiders as nothing more than burdens, but I'm telling you right now, that would be a mistake. We have no way of knowing who we'll be turning away by summarily preventing anyone access to Mercy."

Patty thought of how they could use another doctor, or a nurse, or even someone to run messages around who didn't already have a family in town to take care of. Her friend was right.

"Trevor was a great help at the clinic today," Dr. Olsen added.

Patty knew what was coming and smiled. She didn't mind being wrong about this particular decision.

Melissa looked at Trevor and raised her eyebrows questioningly. "While I wouldn't suggest you work out on the farm, with your allergies, I could certainly use some more help in the clinic."

Trevor was clearly pleased by the praise and Patty watched as the young man blushed and then nodded at the doctor.

Standing again, Patty took a deep breath before walking back to the whiteboard. "Chief Martinez is right that we have a lot of things to cover tonight so I'm going to be blunt. I can see now that I was wrong." She intentionally met Sandy's eyes and held the other woman's gaze, hoping that their friendship wasn't beyond repair. "I made a rushed decision out of fear, and I want this to be an example to us all as to why we can't allow that to happen. We obviously need to protect our resources." Patty looked to Paul then and wasn't surprised to see he was shaking his head. "However, we can't do it blindly. There are more resources than just food and water. Knowledge is power, and although I didn't come up with that brilliant observation, it's something I've always lived by. Sheriff Waters, we'll go ahead with the road block, but let's come up with a sort of vetting system."

Sheriff Waters was hard to read as he squinted while thinking about it. "That could work," he finally said. "Anyone approaching the barricade will be asked their intentions. If they claim to be residents, or family of residents, we'll have them wait while checking out their claims."

"And if they're simply seeking refuge?" Sandy pressed.

"Then we'll have them fill out a form and come before a panel," Patty said. She raised a hand when several people pointed out obvious flaws with the plan. "I know it won't be that simple. Sheriff, can you please put together some ideas as to how we can handle this?"

"Thank you," a small voice rose over the noise.

Patty looked with surprise at Chloe. The girl had a commanding presence, in spite of her size. She reminded Patty what it meant to really survive. "We need to remember what it is we're protecting here," she said to everyone. "It's a way of life, and we can't lose our morality in the process."

Wiping at the board, Patty erased the numbers for the second time that night. With a growing smile, she wrote 652. Turning as she snapped the cap back on the pen, she then pointed it at Chloe. "Welcome to Mercy."

CHAPTER 15

ENERAL MONTGOMERY
Above Peterson Airforce Base, Colorado

"OPEN FIRE, SERGEANT."

"Sir?"

General Montgomery looked over at the sergeant beside him, not surprised by his shocked expression. They were leaning together out of the Huey, a UH-1N helicopter, hovering over the main entrance to Peterson Air Force Base. Below them was a mass of people threatening to break down the barricade that protected the base.

When they first arrived, the sight of a working helicopter had been enough to distract the mob. After they failed to drop supplies and it became apparent the bird wasn't there to help them, the desperate horde had resumed their attempt at looting the base.

"General," Colonel Walsh's voice came over Andrew's headset

and he turned to look at his executive assistant, positioned in the front seat of the Huey. "General, they're civilians."

Colonel Walsh had recently returned from his trip to the nearby FEMA office. He'd confirmed the situation at the base after flying over it on his way back to the mountain an hour before. It was literally being overrun by people fleeing the city of Colorado Springs. The city had a population of almost half a million and the exodus of survivors was something they were unprepared for. General Montgomery already knew what would have to happen, but rather than leave the order up to anyone else, he'd opted to fly out himself.

He looked to the smoldering ruins of the city in the distance and was saddened by the destruction. A large number of fires were still burning and hundreds of useless vehicles blocked the main interstate leading both in and out. While Peterson housed a moderate contingent, it was nowhere near enough to take control of Colorado Springs. They'd be lucky if they could hold their own base. Even if they'd had enough working vehicles, which they didn't, the roads were unpassable.

"You heard me, Sergeant," Montgomery barked, ignoring Walsh. "Give me a line of fire right in front of the main gate. Keep it tight, with minimal casualties. That's an order!" he yelled when the man hesitated.

Reluctantly, the sergeant raised his M16A2 rifle to his shoulder and released a long burst of automatic fire.

General Montgomery watched, expressionless, as eight and then a dozen people collapsed. He couldn't hear the cries, but by the reaction of the people at the head of the mob, there was no doubt that people were screaming as they scattered.

He spoke into his voice-activated headset. "Make the announcement again."

The pilot spoke over the helicopter's PA system, repeating the same statement made when they had first arrived. "Martial law is in effect. The base is under lockdown and no further entry will be allowed. Return to your homes. Disperse immediately or you *will* be shot."

Now that several people had, in fact, been shot, the announcement had more dramatic results. Suddenly, those nearest the fence and barricaded gate were scrambling to fall back, clashing with those still pushing forward. One more burst of random fire solidified the retreat until all that was left near the fence were the unmoving forms of those not lucky enough to get out of the way fast enough.

General Montgomery nodded in satisfaction and changed channels to talk with the commander of the base. "Lieutenant? Inform your men and women at the perimeter that the base is now locked down. Triple your presence at the armed stations. No one leaves or enters. Trespassers are to be shot."

"Yes, sir." The radio communication was scratchy, but clear enough for him to hear the waver in the lieutenant's voice. "What about the bodies, sir?"

"The bodies?"

"At the gate, sir. And the wounded."

General Montgomery motioned for the pilot to head back to the mountain as he stared down at the unmoving forms in question. Behind those were dozens more who were injured in the wake of the stampede to get away from the gunfire. The general clenched his jaw in firm resolution. "Leave them. They'll serve as a stark reminder for those who wish to loot our base." He switched the channel again before the lieutenant could complain and moved back to his seat next to Colonel Walsh.

Walsh removed his headset and stared at him, incredulous.

"We underestimated the situation, Kelly," Andrew sighed, tearing his own headphones off. "It's my fault. I should have been ahead of this. Seen it coming. We can't afford to lose control of the base. Its infrastructure is a critical part of what's left of our limited command. The supplies would have been wiped out in a matter of hours, and the personnel overwhelmed, even if they had the temerity to open fire without orders. It would have eventually jeopardized the mountain, and that can't be allowed."

Kelly looked away without responding and they rode in silence for the rest of the short five-minute ride back to Cheyenne Mountain.

General Montgomery led the way inside the bunker, his shoes clapping against the cool, stone floor. He wondered if the echo mirrored his own soul. Was he to become as cold and hard as the stone in the mountain in order to save it?

Once they had reached a point where they could speak in private, the general turned to his executive assistant, who remained abnormally quiet. "I don't think I need to stress to you now why the FEMA caches must be secured. I know you've only begun to compile a list of active sites, but I want you to issue an order to them immediately."

"To do what?" Colonel Walsh snapped, taking an uncharacteristically bold step toward him.

General Montgomery studied the other man's face for a moment and understood then that he'd likely lost a friend. He forced himself to think of all the black tacks on his wall and it immediately tempered any remorse he might have felt. Much more than friendships would be lost in the coming days. He raised his chin, almost imperceptibly, and his jaw hardened again. "To do whatever is necessary to ensure those caches remain intact. Do I need to remind you, Colonel, that each cache is a minimum of sixty thousand pounds of supplies? Supplies that will be critical in setting up and sustaining the camps capable of housing survivors. For thousands out there, it will be their only salvation."

Colonel Walsh didn't back down, and continued to stare at him with something bordering on loathing. "Sir, with all due respect, we should be saving *all* of those people! Not killing them. You talk about our FEMA camps, but how about we start with the residents of Colorado Springs? Half a million people. Our neighbors. Women and children who only want water and food. They're desperate!"

The general paused before answering. Not because he was unsure of how to respond, but because he needed to make sure the colonel was listening. He knew, historically, if he lost the support of his subordinates, they would ultimately fail in their mission. Humanity would fail, and that wasn't an option. "You're right, Colonel." Walsh looked at him in surprise and he took the opportunity to step in even closer, so that they were mere inches apart. "You're right. They're desperate, and desperate people are dangerous. We're at a critical point, Colonel Walsh. One that, if we have a future, will be noted in history. What we do in these darkest days will determine the fate of the nation. If that means sacrificing some, in order to save the many, then so be it."

When the colonel tried to turn away, General Montgomery grabbed at his arm. It wasn't a gentle motion and it caught the smaller man off guard. Reeling back around, Walsh staggered sideways a step and stared at the general in confusion as he spoke. "I'm counting on you, Kelly."

Kelly made an odd sound before looking away and Andrew believed that the other man was ashamed. Ashamed at his own cowardice and the knowledge that he would never have what it took to make the hard choices. Andrew let him go then, and watched as the colonel took a step before going down to a knee, overcome by the emotional weight of what they would have to do.

"All I'm asking is that you carry out my orders."

Kelly looked up at him then, his face ashen.

"We've all lost loved ones," Andrew said, allowing some emotion to invade his voice. "We're all grieving. Unfortunately,

Colonel Walsh, we're all the hope this country has left. We don't get the luxury of putting our own feelings or wants first. So, *stand up!*"

Colonel Walsh jerked to attention.

"There are still several hours of daylight left, and if you truly want to help those people out there, then you'll get on the radio and start issuing some orders to both our national and state reserves. You can start by deploying the cache at the Denver office, just south of Castle Rock. That's roughly midway between them and Colorado Springs and should be logistically possible. Then, you will have a viable option to offer the survivors attempting to tear down our gates. Understood?"

"Yes, sir." Walsh cleared his throat and met the general's eyes.

While the general wasn't sure if their friendship would remain intact, he had no doubt that the officer would carry out his orders. Watching the other man turn and walk down the long, rocky corridor, he had no regrets over how he'd handled the situation at the base. While a handful of people had unfortunately been killed, it had likely prevented hundreds of other deaths. Though hard to accept, it was a command decision that had to be made and he knew it was only the beginning.

Other sacrifices would have to be made to protect their resources. General Montgomery was willing to go to whatever extremes were necessary.

CHAPTER 16

RUSSELL
Northern Utah, Lakeside

FINE CHINA CLINKED as Russell set his tea cup back on its saucer. He'd always enjoyed a cup of strong Canadian tea. It wasn't the same without a splash of cream, of course, but it was still much more satisfying than plain water or warm soda.

Late afternoon sunshine filtered through lace curtains, dappling the dining room table with intricate patterns. Russell watched the shadows as they moved onto the back of his hand and marveled at the peace of mind it brought him. Such a simple thing, to sit down to a real meal served on proper tableware. He'd found the set in a mahogany hutch and assumed it was normally reserved for holidays and special occasions.

"Today *is* a special occasion," Russell said to the empty house, raising his tea in a solo toast. He'd come across the property at random late that morning, and was somewhat disappointed to find it vacant. He would have rather enjoyed what he imagined would have been an engaging conversation with the homeowners. Based on their choice of furniture and artwork, they were both wealthy and well-traveled.

Smoke wafted inside through the patio screen door, but it wasn't the acrid building fires he'd had to bear over the past week. Rather, it was a sweet-smelling applewood. It had been stacked next to the smoker he'd used to cook his freshly caught trout from a nearby lake.

The fish was half-eaten now, the remnants on a china plater next to a bowl of rice. Some carrots from the garden rounded out his dinner, along with the black tea. Yes. It was a fine meal.

Standing, Russell purposefully walked through the sunlight-laden dining room and into the large family room, his steps muted by a worn oriental rug. A section of built-in bookcases housed a collection of antique toys. "Yes, I would have liked to have met you," he said to the empty room, running his hand along the dusty shelf in front him. It was okay, though, because he had other plans for his evening. Russell smiled.

Pausing in front of an old Fisher-Price record player, Russell pulled one of the plastic records out of the front of the toy, where they were housed. It was identical to a music box he'd had as a child. He set the light blue, thick plastic record onto the turntable and wound up the red knob. His smile broadened as the "teeth" on the yellow arm clicked across the raised notes on the record, the powerless mechanism playing a halting rendition of Edelweiss. One of his favorites.

Closing his eyes, Russell hummed along and imagined himself back in the small attic room of his childhood. Though often hot, the room afforded him a sort of sanctuary for a short time, where he could play his records and daydream about another life.

The music ended and the memory turned dark, invaded by a cloud of torment that had always seemed present, but never showed its face. Russell's smile faded and his eyes snapped open.

He stared at the toy for another heartbeat before reaching out and sweeping it onto the floor. The records scattered, while the box itself stayed intact, much like the thick, cloying presence that could never be shaken.

Russell rolled his shoulders and turned away from the room. He didn't care for it anymore. He'd been able to meditate and think a lot about the state of things, over the past couple of days. About who he was now. The reset button being pushed was a rather liberating phenomenon. Almost enough to compel Russell to believe in a divine plan. Then he realized, or rather, reminded himself that that sort of fallacy was for the weak-minded. He grinned again and began busying himself with clearing the table.

No. He wasn't limited to a story that was already outlined. He was not a protagonist. He was the author of his own destiny, and he knew how it *all* ended.

Setting the soiled dishes into a sink that would never again be full of water, Russell stared out the window above it. It had a lovely view, set high up on rolling plains that were boarded by evergreens.

He'd chosen this house for a reason, because of its proximity to the lake. It was actually a reservoir. A large one, responsible for delivering water and power to the thousands of residents located below it.

A warm summer breeze bent the tall grass in the fields before reaching the house and blowing in through the open window. It was heavy with the scents of both sage and pine. An interesting combination.

Russell focused on the lake. He could see a collection of rowboats and kayaks dotting the surface. The irony that they were no doubt fishing for their evening meal, instead of relaxing on summer vacation, wasn't lost on him. Still, the wooded mountains rising around the clear water offered a view that many would pay good money for.

The lake was full of water, even though it was the middle of summer. Probably because when the power went away, so did the ability to regulate the flow of water. Russell knew this because he'd spent several hours exploring the dam earlier that afternoon. Both the sluice and spillway were closed and had been for the past week. It was an earthen dam. An old one, already in drastic need of maintenance, so it wouldn't take much.

Russell had been a student of many things during his life. While a lot of that was done outside of a classroom, he held three degrees. One of them was in engineering.

Standing at the window, in the proper and antiquated house situated just right on the rolling plain, Russell began to whistle. It was a good day. One full of potential.

He stayed that way for over three hours. He didn't mind waiting. The sun continued its march down the sky, casting longer shadows across the empty dining room table until it reached his feet, near the sink. The light, cheery notes of Edelweiss filled the house, over, and over, and over again, until—

Russell froze, his cheeks puckered, ready to start another round of his favorite tune.

Had the level dropped?

Leaning forward over the sink, Russell squinted at the lake, holding his breath. Yes. Yes, the level was dropping. Quickly.

Russell thought of the residents below the dam, being swallowed up by a wall of water, and the thousands more that would be without a viable reservoir. They were *not* in charge of their destiny. He was.

Russell began to whistle again.

CHAPTER 17

HLOE
Mercy, Montana

"What do you think is going to happen when Hicks and the boys get here?" Ripley asked as she glanced around to make sure no one was listening.

Chloe knew she had a good point. They'd been fortunate to run into Sandy Miller when they did. And if it hadn't been for Bishop's beneficial qualities, Sandy's argument for needing help on the farm might not have been enough to keep them from getting kicked out of Mercy.

Bishop took Ripley's elbow and guided her over to a picnic table so they could all sit down and talk. They were on the outskirts of the main part of town, which consisted of only a few square blocks. It was another picture-perfect Montana summer day masquerading as normal. The small park was across from the only gas station and as their group gathered in it, Chloe wished the coffee stand next to it was up and running. She could *so* use some caffeine.

Trevor settled in between her and Crissy, looking both relieved and stressed at the same time, if that was possible. Bishop and Ripley sat opposite them, placing their backpacks on the table. It was a stark reminder of how close they had all come to leaving and that they were saying goodbye to Ripley.

"We'll deal with that when it happens," Bishop said. "Right now, I'd rather try and talk you into staying."

Ripley shook her head. "Uh-uh. You know full well that if your son were in Helena, or even Butte, you'd already be gone."

Chloe watched as Bishop frowned in response but she wasn't surprised when he didn't try and deny it. She'd be gone, too, if she thought there was a way for her to make it home. However, six hundred miles and three passes made it a daunting mission to even consider. Throw in the fact that she wasn't sure her parents were home when the flash hit, and it made much more sense to wait it out. Although the guy named Caleb talked with Bishop like it was the end of world, she was still holding out hope for things to be fixed at some point.

Chloe looked over at Crissy at the thought of her parents. Her friend wasn't doing well. She was from California, which was a lot farther and the younger girl seemed to be falling into a restless depression.

"And I don't think avoiding the Hicks topic is the way to go," Ripley pressed. She glanced at the teens before looking again at Bishop. "We all know Hicks is a good guy. The boys, on the other hand, are going to be a hard sell."

Bishop waved her off. "I've already mentioned them to Sandy. If they show up, we'll figure it out."

"If?" Crissy spoke up. Her red-rimmed eyes had dark bags under them and her blonde hair had yet to be brushed since reaching Mercy.

Chloe knew that she had a bit of a crush on Jason and as

obnoxious as he was, Crissy didn't need the added anxiety. "They'll be fine." Chloe encouraged, and then reached across Trevor to take one of Crissy's hands, while offering him a weak smile. "We're all going to be fine."

"Melissa—I mean Doctor Olsen—is pretty cool," Trevor stammered. "I hope you guys don't mind me staying with her. It's just that her house is super close to the school, where the clinic is. Plus, I'll have my own room. She's got a big house."

Chloe nudged shoulders with Trevor, pushing him into Crissy. She was happy when it caused the smaller girl to giggle. "Of course we don't mind. We might be able to actually get some sleep at night."

Trevor blushed. "I told you. I don't normally snore. It's my allergies."

"We'll miss you," Crissy promised, clasping onto his arm. "And you better come see us at the ranch as much as possible."

Trevor nodded enthusiastically. "Sure, Crissy. Maybe you can help at the clinic? I can't really picture you wrangling cows."

Crissy giggled again and then wrinkled her nose. "No! But I don't like being around sick people, either. Actually, Sandy has a huge garden she needs help with. My grandma always said I have two green thumbs. Oh! And chickens. Stinky things, but I still like them." Chloe felt some relief to see Crissy smiling again. Maybe she'd be okay if they could keep her distracted.

Ripley had been silently watching the conversation, her expression hard to read. She shifted on the bench so that she was facing Bishop. "Don't worry about me," she urged. "My fiancé is a cop and I know he's out there somewhere. I'll find him, and we'll figure things out. Sandy said we could come back here if it's too dangerous to stay in Helena."

Bishop tilted his head, looking unconvinced. "Why don't you just wait here and see if he turns up? He knows where you were on the hike. If he's as smart as you say he is, he'll figure out this was the nearest place for you to seek refuge."

Ripley squirmed. "Bishop, I'm not going to argue with you, or debate all the possibilities. I think he would be here by now if that were the case, so I'm left with going to *him*. And that's okay. My mind is made up," she urged when Bishop tried to interrupt her. "I'm leaving in the morning. Now, are you all going to walk me to the new Pony Express station or not?"

The group of riders and horses were leaving at first dawn, so it was suggested that Ripley stay the night there. Bishop stood and grabbed both of their packs without comment. Ripley stopped him with a hand on his chest. "Thank you."

As the older man walked off toward the nearby house they'd been directed to, Chloe jumped up and stepped in front of Ripley. Thinking back to early in their trek, before all of their lives had changed, she thought about the simple request the kind woman had made of her. Since then, Chloe had developed a heavy dose of respect for Ripley. To her surprise, Chloe didn't have to force the smile. "Please be careful."

Ripley hugged her, and as they embraced, she whispered near her ear. "Take care of them. Things aren't always what they seem."

CHAPTER 18

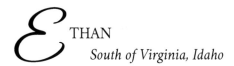
THAN
South of Virginia, Idaho

I DON'T WANT to die.

Ethan kept having the same thought as he sat astride his horse and watched while the two men he'd come to hate debated their next move. They'd reached Charlie's place before nightfall, only to discover that the property was abandoned.

"I told ya, no one's here!" Billy whined. "Now what are we supposed to do?"

Decker kicked at a garbage can, knocking it over. Ethan flinched. He'd almost made a run for it a few hours earlier, but chickened out. He still wasn't sure if they had any bullets left and he kept imagining what it would feel like to have one slam into his back as he rode away. Or, even worse, for his head to explode like the man's did that morning, back in Pocatello.

Charlie didn't keep a very neat house. It wasn't a house, really, but a trailer. A very old trailer with the tires rotting off it and moss growing on the roof. Beer cans littered the ground around a couch that sat outside the front door. It was soiled to the point that Ethan made sure to give it a wide berth.

A dilapidated barn was the only solid structure, although it was missing several boards from the front wall. Decker had just finished looking inside of it and he'd returned empty-handed.

"Charlie must have bugged out and taken the stash with him," Decker said, stepping on beer cans as he made his way around to the backside of the trailer.

Ethan had no idea what the "stash" might be. He figured either drugs or weapons. Maybe both. Either way, Decker was in a foul mood, even for him. They were getting low on food, in spite of his scavenging, and the two didn't seem capable of hunting or fishing. He knew he was becoming more baggage than help, especially since they'd freed themselves.

A pathetic whimper drew his attention over to an oak tree in the front yard. Sliding down off his horse, Ethan took a few steps toward the tree and was dismayed to see a dog cowering in the shade. It was a black lab, difficult to spot in the shadows. There was a stagnant pond nearby that it must have been drinking from, but it was obviously starving to death.

Billy watched him as he moved closer, and Ethan didn't care if it earned him another beating. If he couldn't help himself, or the people they'd killed, he'd at least help the dog. It took a few minutes to work out the knots, but once freed, the dog didn't even look back before scooting off into the bushes.

"What are you doing?"

Ethan jumped at Decker's harsh voice and spun back to find him watching him. "I was just—"

"Get the horses."

"What, we're leaving?" Billy asked, looking annoyed. "After hearing you talk about this place for the past six days, we aren't even staying one night?"

Decker shoved Billy aside as he went past, knocking the smaller man to the ground. "We aren't staying in this trash heap. I wasn't coming here for the accommodations."

"So, where are we going?" Billy rubbed at his hip.

Ethan had already gotten back on his own horse and held the lead ropes to the other two in his hand. He braced himself. If the two got into a fight, it was the shot he was looking for. No pun intended.

Unfortunately, instead of turning back to Billy for an argument, Decker chose to grab Tango's reins. "I'll let you know when I decide. Maybe Vegas."

"Vegas!" Billy awkwardly mounted the other mare. After four days, he still had a hard time getting on the horse. "You know how far that is? Why not just find a nice, empty place close by?"

"I got my reasons." Decker pointed at Billy. "You're welcome to go your own way whenever you want."

Billy hesitated and Ethan realized the smaller man didn't believe Decker would let him leave. He was probably right.

"Nah...Vegas sounds good, man. I'll bet there're all sorts of nice places there ripe for the taking."

Decker turned his attention back to Ethan. "How about you, kid? Ever been to Vegas?" Decker sneered at him then, the same way he'd looked at the farmer right before killing him.

The growing unease in Ethan's chest blossomed. He needed to buy some time. Just one more night. He had to get away before they got too far away from the town of Virginia. If his dad got his note, he'd be looking for him around here. If they went south, he might never find him, and he *knew* his dad was coming for him.

Ethan thought about his mom and stepdad, and the large mansion-like estate they had. "I live there." Decker squinted at him and he did his best not to wilt under the scrutiny. "My stepdad is a computer designer, but he and my mom were gone when...it happened. It's a huge house. With a pool," he added lamely, but Billy wouldn't understand that the pool would soon be unusable without the filter system running.

Vegas was twice as far as it was to Mercy and his mom wouldn't be there, so Ethan had no real reason to want to return. However, if Decker and Billy thought he'd be enough of an asset to take along, he'd live another day. Heck, they might even let their guard down enough if they thought he was on board with the trip that he could actually get away that night. He decided to throw himself into the role.

"I know how to get here," Ethan said with more enthusiasm than he'd shown since the day he was taken. "My dad was bringing me to his place for the summer, but I didn't even want to go. If you help me get home, I'll fish and hunt for you, and you can keep the horses."

Decker's sneer was replaced with a quizzical expression and he stared at Ethan for so long that he thought he'd made a huge mistake and the convict had seen right through his charade. Then, instead of shooting him, he broke out into loud laughter. "So now you want to be our partner? You've got guts, kid."

Billy spat at Ethan as he rode past and it took all of his willpower not to react. "So long as he still cooks and waits on us, I don't care *what* he is," Billy cackled before kicking his horse into a trot.

Decker pulled at Tango's reins as the spirited horse stomped in anticipation of following the mare. "Stay close. It's a long way to Vegas."

Ethan allowed himself to breathe again once they were all moving. He'd managed to extend his usefulness but it didn't change the fact that he was still traveling farther away from his dad. He looked up at the sky and determined twilight was less than an hour away. They wouldn't get that far before stopping.

It turned out to be even less than he'd thought. Twenty minutes later, Billy called out a hello to someone up ahead and

Decker motioned for Ethan to stop. The nausea that was always coiled in the pit of his stomach spread out, threatening to gag him. Whether it was from radiation or stress, Ethan wasn't sure. Whenever they encountered someone, he was terrified they'd end up dead like the trail of others they'd left behind them.

Ethan slowly nudged his horse forward and saw there was a man and woman situated off to the side of the road. They hadn't pitched their tent yet, although their gear was spread out in the grass. They were both squatting down next to a creek that ran within about thirty feet of the interstate.

The middle-aged Hispanic man stood first, eying them cautiously. The woman remained on the ground and Ethan noticed a golden retriever behind her, staying protectively close.

"What's that you got there?" Decker barked, without wasting time on introductions. He was pointing at something the man was holding, and Ethan realized the woman had one, too. Some sort of odd-looking water bottle.

The man hesitated and Ethan's anxiety grew. He edged closer and tried to make eye contact with the man, but he was focused on Decker. He didn't look intimidated and that was bad. Very bad.

"It's just a question," Billy jeered. He was staring hard at the woman.

"They're filters," the woman said, standing. She was somewhat exotic-looking, with long dark hair and a bronzed complexion. She was large for a woman. Bigger than the man she was with.

Billy looked over at Decker, his smile growing. Ethan thought he might throw up. It was horrible timing. He was so close to getting away! He realized then that the woman was looking at *him*. He knew what he looked like, and her expression wasn't hard to read. Understanding... contempt. He gave his head a small shake, trying to discourage her from helping him.

"Really? A filter?" Decker asked. He held out his hand to the man, who was closest to him. "Can I see it?"

"Sorry, we're just getting ready to leave." The man told the obvious lie boldly, inviting Decker to challenge it.

The woman was still studying Ethan. "Are you okay?"

He was tempted to answer her, even though he knew there'd be dire consequences. There was something about her that made him think he'd be safe with her. With them. The dog moved out from behind her and whimpered, as if encouraging him. He didn't get a chance.

"Tell ya what," Decker moved Tango forward several paces until he was less than ten feet from the man. "How about you hand over those water filters and the tent, and I'll ignore your rudeness."

The dog growled as the four adults all held their ground, none of them moving or speaking.

Decker drew his gun.

CHAPTER 19

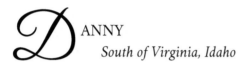

ANNY
South of Virginia, Idaho

DANNY'S NOSTRILS flared as she held herself in check and gauged the men in front of them. Instinct told her they were dangerous, and that the boy didn't belong with them. His face was so battered and bruised that it was difficult to tell how old he was.

The larger man drew a gun.

Danny's eyes flicked toward Sam, who hadn't even flinched, and then back at the boy. He was clearly terrified.

She couldn't allow it to happen. They weren't going to let them go. Even if she thought they would, Danny would never hand over the LifeStraws. Not without a fight.

"How about you take one of the filters?" Sam offered calmly. "We're happy to share."

The man's upper lip curled so that his teeth were bared, reminding Danny of a feral dog. He had dark, lifeless eyes that worried her more than his broad chest and muscular arms. He drew back the hammer on the gun and jostled it slightly. "I'm not going to ask twice."

The creepy little guy was licking his lips while staring at her, but as Sam moved to pick up the filter Danny had left on the ground, he turned to watch him. It was the opening she needed.

Reaching into her back waistband, Danny's hand wrapped around the grip of the Glock. She was relieved she hadn't made a holster yet, and that it was her turn to carry the weapon. While she wasn't an enthusiast, the fire department shared a building with the police department, so Danny had been on several gun range dates with a few of the officers and knew how to handle the weapon.

She drew the slide back as she brought the gun around, and either the sound or movement caught their assailant's attention. He swung his weapon in her direction, but Danny got a shot off first. At less than twenty feet, she wasn't surprised she hit her mark, and watched the bullet impact him in the center of his chest.

"Humph!" The odd sound escaped the man at the same time that he was thrown back in the saddle, the gun falling from his hand.

"Hey!" Creepy Guy shouted, his voice cracking. His horse sidestepped and he grabbed wildly at the saddle horn to keep from falling off.

Sam was already moving, scrambling for the weapon that was now in the dirt on the side of the road. The black and white horse reared as he approached, understandably spooked by the gunshot.

"Whoa," Sam cooed, raising his hands and backing away as the horse screamed in fear, his eyes rolling and ears laid back against his head.

The unmoving man flopped sideways in the saddle, blood already dripping onto the ground beneath him. The horse reared again, then pranced backward, throwing the body so that it hung upside down, its right foot caught in the stirrup.

Danny shifted her focus and turned the Glock on the other man. Hardly a threat, he was canted off to the side of his saddle, hanging on for dear life. The boy was watching it all stoically, and she noticed he was handling his spooked mare without any apparent effort.

"Whoa!" Sam yelled again.

The large quarter horse screamed louder and then bolted, dragging the body alongside it. This spurred the boy into action.

"Ha!" Without hesitation, the teen urged his mount into a gallop and sped after the unsightly scene playing out down the road.

Much to the smaller man's dismay, his own horse followed the others. "Help!" he yelped, while clawing at the horse's mane.

"Grace!" Danny shouted as the dog sprang past them in hot pursuit. Sam snatched the dropped gun before falling in beside Danny, and the two of them ran after the horses.

Less than half a mile down the road, Danny caught up to them. The boy had gotten control of the runaway horse and was standing next to the body. Its foot was still in the stirrup, twisted at an awkward angle, and she didn't need to be a paramedic to know that he was dead.

"Here." The boy was holding the lead rope out to her. His face was still hard to read under all of the abuse, although she thought she saw relief.

"You killed him!" the small, ugly man shouted accusingly at Danny. "You killed Decker." Somehow, the annoying guy had managed to hang on.

"Get off the horse, Billy."

Billy looked at the boy in surprise, obviously shaken by the calm fury in the teen's voice. "Ethan, they killed Decker!"

Danny hung back, putting an arm out to stop Sam from interfering. Grace was circling the group and whining, unsure of the horses.

"I said get off!" Ethan reached out and grabbed the man, yanking him sideways and out of the saddle. The two of them fell to the ground, with the boy on top. Billy was the larger of the two, though clearly at a disadvantage. Danny watched as Ethan straddled Billy and then began to pummel him.

"Oomph!" Billy grunted, as first one fist and then the other landed solidly in his midsection. "Stop, Ethan! Come on, man." He tried to block the strikes as they moved up to his face, but was unsuccessful.

"You killed them!" Ethan growled as he beat the man. "You killed them!"

Danny had seen blind rage before. She could only imagine what had driven the young man to it, but it was time to stop him. He didn't need to add more fuel to his nightmares.

"Come on," Sam barked as they both moved forward and grabbed at Ethan's arms.

"Stop!" Danny ordered when Ethan tried to throw them off. "That's enough!"

Sam managed to wrap Ethan up and hauled him up and off his feet. "It's okay, son," he said, walking several steps away before lowering the teen back to the ground. "It's over. You're okay."

Ethan closed his eyes and took several deep breaths, his shoulders sagging. Sam let him go and moved away as he gave Danny a look of concern.

Danny wished she could give him more time to compose himself, but she needed answers. "Ethan," she said softly. "Who are these guys?"

Ethan opened his eyes and looked over at Billy, who was still on the ground, moaning. "Convicts who escaped their bus when it crashed. He has a gun," he added, gesturing towards Billy. "I don't think he's got any bullets left."

Danny moved over to where Billy lay. He didn't offer any resistance when she pulled his T-shirt up, revealing a small handgun. After confirming it was empty, she stuffed it in her back pocket before rejoining Sam and Ethan. Grace had decided the horses were okay and began edging forward, sniffing at Ethan's hand.

"Are these horses yours?" Sam asked.

Ethan nodded. "Mine and my dad's."

"Where's your dad?" Danny hated to ask the question, except it was getting dark and they needed to quickly decide what they were going to do for the night.

Swallowing hard, Ethan squared his shoulders before looking back over at the dead man. "He shot him, then knocked him out when he tried to stop them from taking our horses. I—" Ethan looked down at the ground. "I don't know if he's alive or not, but I left him a note at...at one of the places we stopped. He'll be looking for me."

Billy struggled into a sitting position and spat blood onto the ground. "What are you gonna do with me?"

Sam studied the man before pointing down the interstate. "I'd suggest you get back on your way."

"Hey!" Ethan objected, taking a step towards the man. "He can't have any of my horses!"

Danny put a hand out on Ethan's chest and smiled at him. "Of course not." She withdrew the Glock and pointed it at Billy. "Unlike yours, this one has bullets in it. Start walking."

"But—"

"Now!" Danny screamed, making Billy jump.

"Can I at least have my bag?" Billy whimpered, looking pleadingly at Ethan.

Ethan moved over to the horse he'd been riding and untied a small duffle bag. He threw it at Billy's feet. "If you come anywhere near me again, I'll kill you."

Billy clasped the bag to his chest and staggered to his feet. Without another word, he spun on his heel and began to stumble south down Interstate 15. They watched until he was beyond where their things were still lying in the grass.

"Thank you." Ethan had taken the black and white horse's lead rope and was stroking his head, further calming him.

Danny smiled in response, struggling to find the right words to say to the boy. She figured there probably really wasn't anything she *could* say. Instead, she turned to Sam. "It's getting dark."

Sam was already on the move. "I'll go get our things together, if you want to move that guy off the road."

It took both Danny and Ethan to wrestle Decker's deformed leg out of the stirrup and then maneuver his body into the grass. Sam arrived carrying both packs on his shoulders, while awkwardly walking the bikes, as they were tossing a couple of broken tree branches over Decker.

"Billy disappeared around the next bend," Sam offered, dropping the gear and bikes onto the ground. "I don't think he'll be bothering us."

It was getting hard to see, so Danny knelt down and dug around in her pack until she found their sacred flashlight. When she clicked it on, Ethan gasped in shock.

"How?" the boy asked. "Where you came from, does stuff still work?"

Danny felt guilty for not explaining it first. "No, I'm sorry. From what we know, the flash might have affected the whole world. We figured out certain flashlights work, if they didn't have batteries in them during the event."

Clearly disappointed, Ethan still smiled at the light. He reached out his hand, passing it through the beam as if it were some sort of liquid gold. "Well, I'm still stoked to see it."

"Where were you when these cowards attacked you?" Danny asked, regretting the question when it made the boy's smile fade.

"It's been four days." Ethan bent down and began to pet Grace. The dog pushed up against him until he sat so she could get into his lap. He laughed at the retriever's antics but then grew serious again as he thought back over the four days. "We were north of Idaho Falls, at a rest stop."

Sam whistled. "That's quite a distance. Does your dad still have a horse?"

Ethan shook his head.

"You said he was shot," Danny pressed. "Do you know how bad it was?"

His brows furrowed; Ethan pressed his lips together. "I don't think it was too serious. Looked like his arm or shoulder was hit. He was knocked off his horse when it happened, but he got back up and was conscious and everything. He still tried to stop them, and that was when Decker hit him in the head with his gun. He was going to shoot him—I talked Decker out of it."

As Ethan recalled what happened, Danny was reminded that in spite of his size, they were dealing with a scared teenager, not an adult. They couldn't just leave him out there, alone. "How old are you, Ethan?" she asked.

"Fifteen. I'll be sixteen next month," he added, as if age still mattered in the new world.

Fifteen. Danny closed her eyes. He was even younger than she'd thought. His strength and perseverance were impressive. She turned to Sam and when their eyes met, she knew he was thinking the same thing. She gave a small nod of agreement.

"Ethan," Sam said, moving to sit down next to him on the ground, with Decker's body cooling less than twenty feet away. "I don't know where you're heading, but if you're going back to where you were last with your dad, it's the same direction as us. I think we'd be better off if we all stuck together."

Ethan's hand stopped moving on Grace's head as he looked over at Sam, and then up at Danny. His green eyes were still visible in the gathering dark and they were wet with unshed tears. "Will you help me find my dad? We were on our way home. We have to get home to Mercy."

Danny's breath caught and she was filled with such a feeling of purpose that it was almost overwhelming. Kneeling down on the other side of Ethan, she put her hand over top of his, still resting on Grace's head. "Yes," she said, her voice barely more than a whisper. "And Ethan—"

Ethan took a shuddering breath and stared at her expectantly.

"Do you believe in fate?"

CHAPTER 20

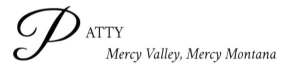

$\mathcal{P}$ATTY
Mercy Valley, Mercy Montana

THE ROOSTER CROWED as Patty put another egg in her basket. The sun was just beginning to peek over the ridgeline of the mountains to the east, and she enjoyed the last few minutes of coolness she would experience for the day

She snatched another egg and then jumped away from the rooster, just in time to avoid a nasty scratch. "Ornery old cuss," she muttered. If they didn't need more chickens, he would have been the first on her kill list. "We can still make it happen," she snapped as the bird lunged at her again.

"You need to stand up to him," Caleb chuckled. "You've allowed that bird to chase you around one too many times."

Patty shoved the basket of eggs at her husband. "I thought you were going to sleep in," she said, ignoring his advice.

Caleb shrugged. "I'm tired enough to sleep for a couple of

days straight, but whenever I close my eyes, numbers and lists start scrolling."

Patty turned her attention to the vegetable garden that was becoming overrun with weeds. It certainly didn't take long. Even with getting such an early start to the day, she wouldn't have enough time to make more than a dent in the work needed to be done around the place.

"I'm so tired, Patty."

Patty paused, the weariness in Caleb's voice startling her. He hadn't come out to the hen house to tease her about roosters. Pulling her gloves off, she stuck an arm through his and guided him over to what she called her "thinking bench". Situated toward the back of the property, it sat up on the sloping acres with a nice view of the valley. Sitting, Patty stared out at the soft light spilling along the mountain slopes. It all looked so…normal.

"We're going to have to take a few days and work on getting things in order at our own house," Caleb observed. "I'll need to start chopping wood soon, if we hope to have enough to get through the winter." Fortunately, they had a wood-burning fireplace.

"I was thinking I might ask Sandy if that young girl might be able to help us for a day," Patty said. "Chloe, I think her name is. We could trade some apples or something."

"She reminds me of you."

Patty laughed. "Really?"

"When you were younger," Caleb explained. "You had the same sort of tenacity and spunk. I think it's a good idea."

"Aaron and the others should be on their way out of town by now." Patty squeezed Caleb's arm. "It was a good idea. The Pony Express."

"We'll see how it pans out. Meanwhile, I've made some new contacts."

Patty's brow creased. He didn't appear optimistic about it.

"More bad news?" She wondered why he hadn't mentioned it sooner.

Caleb leaned back on the bench, his face profiled by the fresh sunlight. His expression was hard to read. "More of the same. But, one of them claims to be with the US military."

Patty gawked at him, turning on the bench to face him. "What? When? You should have told me!"

Caleb shook his head. "I wasn't sure, Patty. It was the right frequency, but obviously anyone with some basic knowledge could get on there and make the same assertion."

"Why are you telling me now?" Patty asked, not certain she wanted the answer.

"Because last night the contact told me they're activating what's left of the national and state guards. It sounds like there might be some sort of loose order coming together at some point. I thought we could get the stranded kids' names to them. I imagine they'll be creating lists of survivors, same as in any other mass causality incident, for reuniting loved ones."

The news of an existing government was huge. The fact that Caleb hadn't been forthcoming about it was troubling, though. "What's wrong, Caleb?"

Caleb hmphed and tilted his head at her, looking incredulous. "You have to ask?"

She squinted at him until he looked away. "You know full well what I mean, Caleb. You're a Vietnam veteran who's dealt with more death than I did in my thirty years of nursing. I know you can handle stress. I know you, more than anyone, are capable of facing what we're up against. So, I'll ask you again. What's wrong?"

"I've seen what sorts of decisions we've already had to make," Caleb said, looking grim. "I suspect it's only going to get harder and I don't know if the government is going to necessarily have our best interest in mind."

"Shutting off Mercy is the right thing to do," Patty said, not expecting to have to defend that particular decision to her husband.

"I know it is," he countered. "I said it was hard, not wrong. But what about when supplies start to run low? Or if we can't get the water distribution worked out?"

Patty looked away, back out over the valley. She didn't have an answer.

"I heard you talking with Melissa," Caleb pushed when she remained silent. "People are already running out of their medicine, and some of them will die without it. She has some of it in stock, but who's going to determine how to disperse it? Will it be based on age, need, or who contributes most to the community? Maybe you'll hold a lottery? That sounds familiar."

"Stop!" Patty gasped. Standing, she turned her back on Caleb and hugged herself. That wasn't a conversation she was prepared to have.

"This isn't something that can be avoided," Caleb pushed, sounding angry. "What are you going to do, form another committee? Because I hope you'll put in a good word for me."

Patty choked back a sob and spun on him. "That isn't fair!" she yelled. She knew he was referring to the blood thinner medication she'd given him the night before. "You're vital to Mercy. We can't lose you."

Caleb pulled her close then and wrapped her up in a tight hug. She cried against his chest, not caring for the moment if she appeared weak or vulnerable. No one else was there. This was her Caleb. If she couldn't be transparent with him, if she'd already lost herself, then she might as well just walk off into the mountains, because none of it would be worth fighting for.

"Chief Martinez and Tane Latu are going to help me set up some transponders this afternoon," he said into her hair once she fell silent. "If we can get them working with line-of-sight, we should be able to establish handheld radio contact within the valley."

Patty took a cleansing breath and centered her emotions. She felt better. Having a good cry always helped and she was thankful to have someone she could trust and lean on. Looking up, she offered Caleb a weak smile, happy for the change in subject. "I thought all of that stuff was blown."

Stepping back, Caleb took her hand and they walked down to the garden. With the sun rising, the heat was already starting to seep in. "Tane has some electronics background. When he was talking about the radios with the fire chief, they ended up taking one of the handhelds apart and, long story short, Tane was able to cannibalize enough parts to get a few working. The chief had some brand-new, out of the box without batteries in them, so I guess it wasn't too difficult," Caleb explained. "The transponders are a lot harder, but Aaron brought him back a couple things from Helena that Tane needed and he thinks we might be in luck now."

"This is great!" Patty threw some weeds off to the side and thought about the implications. Logistics was one of their bigger problems, as far as time went. She spent nearly half the daylight hours riding to and from their house, and all over town, just to talk with people and spread information. If they actually re-established instant communication, even limited, it would be a huge step forward. She wondered again why she was just now hearing about it, but then realized that he'd been sound asleep when she'd arrived home the night before. She'd slept at city hall for three out of the past four days. Even though their world had been instantly reduced with the flashpoint, the terrain was suddenly bigger and more difficult to traverse, and everything took more time to accomplish.

"I spoke to Al last night," Patty offered, excited to add her own good news to the conversation. "He gave me a list of parts he needs that I passed on to Aaron. With them, he might be able to get a motorcycle running."

Caleb paused with a weed in his hand as he thought about it. "We'd need to work on getting some of the roads cleared, and of course fuel is scarce, but it would certainly be good to have in cases of emergencies."

"It's been a week," Patty realized. "A week today since the flashpoint. I know we're a long way off from being okay. Regardless, at least we're managing better than most, based on all the information you've gathered."

"Not all of us in Mercy are," Caleb countered.

Patty yanked at a particularly tough weed and thought it much like the hold-outs Caleb was referring to. "Right." It came loose with a large clump of dirt and she shook it out to fill the hole back in. "While I understand why some people don't want to be a part of our collaborative effort, they're going to pose a problem eventually."

"It's over fifty people, Patty." Caleb grabbed a hoe and went to work on the wider aisles. "What happens when some of them realize they can't go it alone and come to you for water or food?"

Patty leaned back on her heels and peered up at Caleb. "We're making it very clear to them that if they chose not to be a part of our interworking community now, there won't be an option to do so later."

"'...we understand only the individual's capacity to make sacrifices for the community, for his fellow man.'" Caleb leaned on the hoe while he spoke.

Patty knew her husband well enough to catch the undercurrent of the saying, but she still had to ask. "What's that from?"

Caleb stared at her stoically before answering. "Adolph Hitler, from the manifesto *Mein Kampf.*"

Patty's face reddened. "You're comparing me to Adolph Hitler?"

"No, Patty. Of course not." Caleb dropped the garden tool and knelt down in front of her. "I just want you to remember, throughout all of this, that sometimes it's easier to side with the 'greater good'. To let a committee handle a difficult decision so you can wipe your hands of it and we can theoretically sleep better at night."

Patty tried to pull away when he reached for her hand, but he grabbed on tight and pulled her closer. "I don't know what you want from me," she insisted.

Caleb shook his head. "I want you to follow your heart. You're a good person, and sometimes, what looks better on paper and reads well in a meeting isn't the *right* choice."

Conflicted, Patty struggled to grasp his meaning. Then, she thought about Chloe's face in the meeting yesterday, and her reservations when she saw the young man given an inhaler. She thought about Melissa silently handing her the bottle of blood thinner pills for Caleb. She imagined Old Man Summers sitting alone up in his cabin at the end of the road, refusing to be a part of anything. He'd lost his wife a couple of summers ago and hadn't been the same since. Would she deny him water if he asked for it a month from now?

"Keep your committees," Caleb urged, watching her face as the emotions played out across it. "Just make sure that everyone knows who their leader is. So that when the hard calls come, when the *really* hard ones need to be made, they'll still listen to you."

CHAPTER 21

ENERAL MONTGOMERY
Cheyenne Mountain Complex, Colorado

THE PICTURE WAS CREASED and faded, having traveled the world in the general's suitcase for more than twenty years. He sat staring at it, alone in the bunker meeting room, deep below Cheyenne Mountain. It had been what...three years since he'd looked at it? The young, attractive woman with honey-colored hair glowed with happiness. She *had* been happy then, cuddling their son to her chest. They'd been married for less than five years and she had no idea what sort of life they were staring down the barrel at.

Andrew traced his son's face with a finger, trying to memorize it. How long would it be before he forgot what he looked like? Most of the current pictures of him were all digital. Stored on his phone or online. That was all gone now. In a blink, his grandchildren were all but erased from his world.

Clearing his throat, Four-star General Andrew Montgomery straightened in his seat and dropped the photo into the bottom drawer of the desk he sat at. They had all suffered a great loss, but he didn't reach his rank or position by being a committed husband or father. His wants and needs came after those of the nation. That would never change.

Janice finally divorced him after he'd made general yet still refused to retire. When he'd accepted the new position at USNORTHCOM five years ago, she went to New York instead. He glanced up at the map on the wall and all of the red marks on the east coast, including New York, then pulled a stack of papers in front of him. There was work to be done.

Barely twenty-four hours since the shooting at the base, and Walsh already had hours' worth of data for him to pour over. Sighing, he saw by the old-fashioned clock on the wall that it was only ten in the morning. Maybe he'd get his second cup of coffee before delving into it. Before he had a chance to stand, there was a knock at the door, followed by Walsh entering without waiting for a response.

"Sir," Walsh said formally, moving to stand in front of the desk. "Did you have a chance to look through my reports yet?"

Andrew studied the other man for a few seconds before answering. There was a strained formality between them that hadn't been there since they first started working together several years before. "No, Colonel, I was just about to start. Perhaps you can hit the highlights?"

Walsh took a seat and folded his hands in his lap, still avoiding any direct eye contact. "I've reassigned personnel as requested, to both Peterson and the FEMA office in Denver. There haven't been any further…incidents."

General Montgomery tilted his head at the comment but didn't respond to it as he sat back down and rifled through the papers. "Status of the caches?"

"We're using the chopper to drop the pallets at what we're calling Camp One, located midway between Colorado Springs and Denver. The deployment is already underway, with over two dozen boots on the ground. But..."

The general looked up expectantly. "Yes?"

"Sir, you saw for yourself how many people are fleeing the cities. There's a lot of thirsty, hungry, sick, and scared refugees on the seventy miles of interstate between Denver and Colorado Springs."

"Which is why it's an ideal location for the camp," General Montgomery said evenly.

"Right, and as soon as that bird started dropping pallets early this morning, it was like a beacon. We're facing a situation similar to what we saw at Peterson yesterday, unless we figure out a way to control the influx of refugees. I simply don't have the manpower to control them. It's going to take days to deploy the tents and equipment. Right now, my soldiers are reduced to handing out bottled water and protein bars to deter them from rioting."

"No," General Montgomery said with some force, causing Walsh to look at him sharply. "If we handle our emergency resources like a soup kitchen, we'll never establish any shelters before they're overrun. We'll be back at square one."

"Then what do you suggest?" Walsh's voice rose an octave. "Do I have to remind you that these people are becoming more desperate by the hour and we're the only ones offering any sort of lifeline?"

"It would seem that I am the one who needs to remind *you* of what our mission is." The general leaned forward then, doing his best to speak with a level tone. "This isn't a short-term crisis. If we treat it that way, we'll lose what little tactical advantage we have and all will be lost, Colonel. We won't be able to recover, at least not fast enough to save the thousands of people who are out there right now dying a slow death."

Colonel Walsh leaned forward then also, so that their elbows almost met in the middle of the desk. "That's the issue, sir. These caches were never meant as long-term solutions. They're geared to keep a task force and limited number of survivors self-sufficient for seventy-two hours, and can be extended to fourteen days with assistance. We're already supplementing Camp One with supplies from the mountain to broaden its scope, but it's still not going to be enough to meet the needs of what they're seeing out there."

General Montgomery sat back and picked up a pen, tapping it on the top paper while working the problem. It was two-fold: a lack of control and supplies. It called for extreme measures. His pen stopped moving. "Set up a military exclusion zone."

"Sir?"

"Martial law has already been declared, making our recovery a military operation. The camps will all be handled as military exclusion zones. I want your soldiers to establish the boundaries of the camp and then shut down Interstate 15 both north and south of its borders."

"Roadblocks?" Walsh looked skeptical.

"There might not be working vehicles, but people are still using the road to travel," the general said with some frustration. "Until the camp is set up and can be properly secured, no one passes through. I'll arrange to have water stations established so we can at least offer that much."

Walsh nodded. "That might work. Although the logistics to erect enough of a roadblock to keep anyone from simply walking around will be a challenge."

Andrew tried not to groan out loud. He had a growing sense of disappointment in the colonel's ability to think for himself. "It doesn't have to contain the whole camp, at least not at first. Use whatever local resources are available to create fences. Refugees will have the option to turn around, or walk around, and if they try and enter, they will be met with swift repercussions."

"Meaning?"

"Non-lethal force will be used first, and if that fails, lethal measures are authorized." General Montgomery squinted at Walsh. "It'll work. Once we're able to offer shelter and meet their basic needs, we'll gain control, but we must establish authority *now.*"

"I'll go to the site myself after we're done here and oversee it," Walsh replied. "If we can work with some of the local residents, we might be able to get some help with the fencing in exchange for food."

"Good," General Montgomery said crisply. "Excellent idea. As you already pointed out, these shelters are temporary fixes. We need to always be looking at our long-term objective."

"Which is? Realistically, I mean," Walsh added when the general glared at him. "Obviously, we want to eventually assure the survival of as many people as possible. We aren't going to accomplish that with these camps. We don't have any other supplies coming, which means when it runs out, we're restricted to local resources. We'll need working farms, permanent shelters, and natural reservoirs."

"I've already got personnel researching those options," General Montgomery said. "Based on your reports from our own state and others, most major cities, or even those of moderate size, aren't habitable."

"No," Walsh confirmed. "You know we've only had continued contact with the western and some central states. We have to assume that anyone south or east of Nebraska is either already dead, or will be, from gamma radiation, so we aren't even talking about them. The rest of us? Between fires, accidents, illness, riots, and now lack of water or starvation, places of high population aren't livable. We're already seeing water-borne illnesses cropping up and thousands are dying from simple dehydration."

"What about state and local government resources?" the general asked.

Walsh reached out and thumbed through the top two pages on the general's desk. "Here," he directed, pulling one aside. "This lists the state guard's we've had contact with and their status. And this one," he pulled the next sheet out. "These are the county department of emergency managements we've also spoken to. Well, not literally, of course. It's all through ham radio controllers."

General Montgomery glanced down at the abysmal lists. With upwards of fifteen states that should still be viable, they were concerningly short. "Issue the same directive to all of them. I realize that some are civilian, but since we're under martial law we can work to get military contingents assigned at all levels. Number each camp by state designation and require daily reports."

Walsh squirmed in his seat. "There's going to be some pushback from the local governments that are still functioning, and Vice Admiral Welling isn't going to be happy about it. He's demanding a meeting again, sir."

"I don't care about anyone's feelings or territorial claims," the general barked. "Remind them that if they want our continued support, they'll comply." He squeezed the bridge of his nose to literally push back against the tension headache that grew stronger at the mention of the vice admiral. He was the Deputy Commander of USNORTHCOM prior to the flashpoint and had been a thorn in his side ever since he declared martial law. "There's already a scheduled meeting of the joint staff this evening. Whatever he has to squabble about can wait until then."

"Yes, sir," Walsh said in a drawn-out way that indicated they both knew the vice admiral wouldn't be happy. "What kind of continued support can we offer the local governments?" Walsh asked, getting back to business. "Yeah, our initial caches are larger than theirs, and we have some working machinery, but this will come down to food and medical supplies."

"I'm sending out teams to Mount Weather and Raven Rock."

Colonel Walsh sat back in his chair, stunned. "Sir, those caverns are nothing more than mass graves now. You know we had radio confirmation that they were all dying from acute radiation exposure on the *first* day. No amount of rock could protect them from gamma radiation."

"You're being short-sighted again, Colonel!" General Montgomery reprimanded. "Mount Weather was FEMA's emergency operations center. There's a literal treasure-trove of caches there. Since Raven Rock is so close to them, and housed upwards of five thousand government employees, it stands to reason they might be worth a visit, too."

"They're tombs," Walsh insisted. "And they're more than fifteen hundred miles away. Not to mention the logistical nightmare of moving the caches once we have them."

"Those are the details I'll leave up to you," General Montgomery said. "It's part of our long-term solution. Figure it out. There's also a document we need to retrieve from Mount Weather."

Walsh, clearly unhappy, crossed his arms over his chest. "The Survivor's List."

Montgomery nodded. The Survivor's List was a compilation of six thousand five hundred key people, with names and addresses, considered vital to the survival of the nation should a catastrophe or apocalypse strike.

"There's a fair amount of personal at Ellsworth Air Force Base in South Dakota," Walsh replied. "They're slightly closer and more than capable of deploying some recon for us. I can get them to the mountain to retrieve the list and then come up with a plan to move the supplies."

"Make it happen." General Montgomery stacked the papers back up and then hesitated, knowing that Walsh would resist his next order. He glanced down at the drawer where he'd dropped the picture. There were going to be a lot more sacrifices needing to be made. "We'll need to establish supply lines."

Walsh pointed at the papers that were now in a neat pile. "I highlighted the locations I thought were most central for each state. It's not much, but we have to start somewhere."

The general didn't bother looking at the list. "Right. The locations are good, but the how is what's more important right now."

"We've got more vehicles than anyone else," Walsh admitted. "For all the good it does us. It'll take weeks and more manpower than we have to clear the roads before anything can get through, even locally."

"Horses."

"Sir?"

"Going back to basics, Colonel." The leather seat squeaked as General Montgomery rose and walked over to his map. He waved a hand at it. "Back when our military was first founded, we used horses for everything from transportation to war. I don't think it's too far of a stretch to suggest we do it again. It'll be years before we get a working infrastructure back in place, and much longer than that until we have the means to manufacture needed mechanical equipment, or even produce fuel."

"I've had some men using them already to travel back and forth between the base and the mountain." Walsh frowned. "How do you suggest we implement their use in a broader sense? It's not like we can go purchase them."

General Montgomery turned and leveled Colonel Walsh with a stern look.

"You want us to take them."

"I have the authority to requisition private property."

Walsh hung his head. "Yes, sir."

"And Colonel Walsh?"

He looked up reluctantly.

"Let's not call them camps, but shelters. I wouldn't want to give the wrong impression."

CHAPTER 22

CHLOE
Miller Ranch, Mercy, Montana

CRISSY WAS STILL in bed even though it was almost noon. Chloe was still worried about her and was going to make sure Trevor came to the ranch a lot since Crissy laughed more with him around.

Chloe's bare feet slapped against the hardwood floor as she crossed the large main room of the log house. She paused in front of the bookcase that held the photo of Sandy's son and grandson. Ethan was the kid's name, and although he looked as old as Chloe in the picture, Sandy said his sixteenth birthday was in a few weeks. She tugged at the Star Wars T-shirt she was wearing. She was over feeling weird about wearing Ethan's old clothes because there wasn't much to choose from. Her jeans still had some life left in them, at least.

Ethan's dad was a big man, and pretty much fit the rugged cowboy cliché perfectly. She hoped for Sandy's sake that they were on their way home like she repeatedly insisted. Caleb Woods, the mayor's husband, told her last night after the meeting that he would get her name on a survivors list. He was some sort of radio guru and was talking with a bunch of other people all over the world, including the military in Washington state. He said that when her parents looked for her, they'd be able to learn where she was, and come for her. She appreciated how he'd used the word "when", instead of "if".

Her stomach cramped as the invasive, negative thoughts of not knowing where her parents were threatened to take over. Turning from the picture, she decided she needed something to take her mind off her own family.

The notebook Sandy had drawn her sketch in of the lake and cow pasture was still on the kitchen counter. Chloe took it and went out onto the back patio. Squinting, she looked out at the rolling green fields that met the steep mountain slope in the distance. Caleb and Sandy were out doing something with the cows while she'd been hauling water in from the pump for a bath. She'd felt sort of guilty, knowing that there were probably a ton of people out there who didn't even have any to drink, but it had been almost two weeks since she'd bathed in clean water and it was *so* needed. She didn't bother to heat it up. Aside from it taking too long, it was so hot out, that the cool water felt good.

"You sure smell better."

Chloe jumped at Bishop's voice and turned to see him standing in the open patio door. "Well, you won't need to stand upwind of me, now," she laughed and then waved her hands over her shirt. "And the force is with me."

Bishop smiled and then pointed at the notebook. "Sandy showed that to me earlier. It's a good idea, but will take a lot of legwork."

Chloe shrugged. "I've got time."

"Thomas and Ethan can help when they get back," Sandy

added, from astride a tall black horse. She'd just come around the corner of the house, and the lead rope for another horse was in her other hand. "Do you know how to ride, Chloe?"

Chloe stared up at the massive beast and bit at her bottom lip nervously. "Umm...no, not really. I attempted it once at camp a couple of years ago, and it ended badly."

"Well, this gal's name is Lady, and she won't give you any trouble." Sandy slid out of the saddle with such a fluid motion that Chloe was surprised when she landed next to her.

"You want me to ride...her?" Lady was mostly white with some black spots and probably considered average-sized, Chloe guessed. She was much shorter than Sandy's horse and her back had a bigger dip in it. She looked old.

"Here," Sandy instructed, handing the rope to Chloe. "Let's start with walking them for a bit. Then, we'll graduate to sitting in the saddle."

Chloe wasn't convinced it was such a good idea, but didn't want to disappoint Sandy. Taking the rope, she cautiously moved around the horses and fell in beside the rancher as they led them out of the yard.

"Have fun!" Bishop called, chuckling.

"Where are we going?" Chloe asked when they approached the barn.

"The lake," Sandy answered without preamble. "I want you to see it. Here," she handed her lead rope to Chloe. "Hold this for a moment."

Chloe stood awkwardly staring at the horses while Sandy ran into the barn. She was in the exact same position when the older woman returned a few minutes later, carrying fishing poles and a tackle box.

Laughing, Sandy set the gear down and rested a hand on Chloe's shoulder. "You have nothing to fear," she promised. "Treat them like a friend and they'll be yours for life. Oh, and giving them treats doesn't hurt, either." She took two carrots out of her back pocket and gave one to Chloe.

Taking the carrot, Chloe stared at it and then Lady. "What if she bites my fingers?"

"Oh my goodness." Sandy shook her head. "Do it like this." She lay her carrot in the palm of her hand and held it out to the black horse, who daintily accepted the treat.

Encouraged, Chloe copied her, and giggled when the hairs on Lady's lips tickled her palm. The horse stretched her head out and nudged at Chloe's chest, clearly wanting attention. Tentatively at first, she stroked the horse's long, glossy neck. When nothing horrible happened, she moved on to Lady's cheek and within a few minutes, the horse had won Chloe over her and she didn't think Lady was going to bite her head off.

"See?" Sandy cooed. "Gentle as a kitten. Do you know how to fish?"

Chloe looked up and then stumbled back when Lady pushed against her for more attention. Laughing, she was glad that she wouldn't come across as completely helpless. "Yes! I used to go fishing all the time with my dad. Trout, mostly, but we got some salmon a couple times, too."

"Excellent," Sandy replied. "Let's go catch dinner!"

Fifteen minutes later they were partway down a trail through the back field, with Chloe on Lady's back. She clutched the saddle horn tightly, but she was quickly warming up to the experience. Her legs were so short that Sandy had to adjust the stirrups all the way up, and she understood why cowboys wore boots. After getting over her initial fear, she found being up on the animal's back exhilarating and didn't resist when Sandy picked up the pace.

It took almost half an hour to reach the small lake and Chloe realized long before getting there that saying the project required a lot of legwork was a massive understatement. It had to be a good two miles, minimum, and although it would be flowing downhill, that didn't diminish the amount of piping it would take.

The sun was high overhead, heating the day up into the nineties again. An eagle soared among tall evergreens lining the far shore, which was nestled up against the mountain. It was there that the land began a sharper pitch and the last of the open fields disappeared into thick woods.

Chloe had already fallen in love with the land, and the new vista only strengthened her desire to help the ranch succeed. Twisting in the saddle, she looked out over what was becoming an increasingly epic view of the valley. When she turned back, she discovered that Sandy had stopped up ahead and was shielding her eyes as she stared at something on the lake.

The lake itself was around five to eight acres, fed by upper mountain runoff. Since it wasn't that large, it was easy to see that three men were fishing near the far end of it, and had a tent pitched nearby. Chloe recognized the tent.

Sandy was reaching behind her to untie her rifle when Chloe came alongside her. "I think I know who it is."

Sandy hesitated and was about to ask a question when one of the men called out to them first. "Hello!"

Chloe studied the figure as he took several steps in their direction. Behind him, another man was sitting on the ground, half-turned from them, while a third was just coming out of the tent. She assumed one of them was Hicks. "Jason?" she yelled back. While she couldn't stand the guy, she was still relieved to know he was okay. Also, if he was there, then that probably meant Hicks, Ben, and Adam were, too. She didn't have time to process why they were up at this lake, instead of in town.

Sandy did, though. "This your other group of missing friends?" she asked, while still untying her rifle.

Chloe watched as the rancher she'd come to respect moved with an intensity she didn't understand.

"How about you stop what you're doing there?"

Chloe looked back to see that the man who'd come out of the tent was moving quickly past Jason and toward them. It wasn't Hicks, and he had something in his hand. It took Chloe a moment to realize it was a gun and confusion clouded her mind as she watched the other man stand, also a stranger.

"You're welcome to the fish," Sandy called back, having moved her hands away from the rifle and then out in front of her. "This is my property. Sandy Miller," she said, as if introducing herself at a dinner party. "And you are?"

"In need of a way out of this valley," the man rebutted, as he continued to close the space between them.

Jason followed, his gaze never leaving Chloe. A torrent of questions raced through her mind, but she knew better than to ask most of them. Instead, she chose the most obvious. "Jason, what are you doing?"

Jason stopped a few feet from Lady and stared up at Chloe with a sneer. "Whatever it takes."

Before she could come up with a smart retort, there was a whizzing sound and then Jason's face contorted in pain as the thick end of a fishing pole slapped across the back of his legs.

"Argh!" Jason cried out as he dropped to his knees.

"What—" the man with the gun began to shout as he turned toward Jason, but their rescuer was already stepping over Jason and moving in his direction.

He slammed into the assailant while grabbing at his wrist and wrenching the weapon away at the same time. Leaning back, he followed through with what Chloe could only describe as a total kung fu move, kicking him squarely in the chest.

"Oomph!" Flying backwards, unarmed and gasping for breath, the man landed hard in the dirt.

It all happened so fast, that Chloe hadn't even moved in her saddle. Mouth hanging open, she watched as the man flipped the gun around in his hand like a baton and pointed it at the third, unarmed assailant. He was staring down the barrel, in shock, with what Chloe figured was the same expression as her.

"I'd suggest you don't move," the man advised, gesturing with the gun for him to move away from Sandy's horse.

Chloe let out her pent-up breath, gasping in astonishment. "Bishop!"

CHAPTER 23

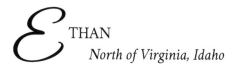

THAN
North of Virginia, Idaho

ETHAN PEDDLED the bike with less enthusiasm as they got farther north of the small town called Virginia. He knew it was a huge longshot that his dad found the note he'd left tucked into the dead farmer's pocket, but it was all he had. Aside from thinking he'd find his dad's corpse rotting back at the rest stop where they were attacked, Ethan chose to believe he was out there looking for him.

He glanced back at Sam, who was riding the other bike, with Grace trailing diligently behind him. Ethan had gladly offered to let Danny ride Tango. It was obvious, even to him, that she wasn't a hundred percent. The night before, after they'd made camp a reasonable distance from where they'd dumped Decker, she'd told him some of their story. He understood why she didn't go into too much detail…he didn't, either. It was too hard to dredge up the memories, when they deserved to stay buried.

Ethan told them, twice, that he wanted to wait for his dad near the town. That he didn't want to get too far away, but neither Sam or Danny had committed to stopping. His stomach twisted. The thought of watching them ride away and leaving him behind was almost enough to compel him to keep moving. Almost.

"Hey, Danny?" he finally built up the nerve to call out. "Do you think maybe we could stop soon?"

She reined Tango in, and Ethan pulled up beside the horse on the mountain bike. Danny looked like a natural in the saddle, although she'd claimed not to have very much experience with riding. It was probably more about having a natural connection with animals. They could sense when you were afraid of them, especially horses. That's why Billy never got the hang of it.

Danny looked up at the sun, gauging what time of the day it was. Ethan guessed it was around two in the afternoon. Still tons of daylight left. "My dad," Ethan urged. "I just want to camp out on this road for the next day or two. I promise, if he doesn't come, then I'll keep riding with you and we can all use the horses. You won't need the bikes anymore."

"We don't want to take your horses, Ethan," Sam said, stopping alongside him. "And we definitely don't want you out here by yourself." The older man looked up at Danny then, and raised his eyebrows questioningly at her.

"Oh, right!" she gasped, realizing Sam was looking at her to back him up. "Of course not. It's just that I have to get home to my dad, too. He's going to need some medication for his heart soon."

Ethan kicked at a rock on the road. "Do you have the medicine for him?"

Danny shifted in the saddle, the leather creaking. Tango's tail swished, swatting at a battalion of flies. "No. I'm hoping I might be able to find some along the way."

"I'm really good at scavenging for things!" Ethan offered enthusiastically. "I swear. Decker and Billy had me sneaking into all sorts of places. I got really good at it."

Danny looked crestfallen and then glanced guiltily at Sam. "Ethan, you don't have to do that for us. You don't have do anything to stay with us. Of course, we can wait here for a day or so for your dad. I just want to make sure you understand why we can't stay here any longer than that."

Ethan nodded, filled with an immense relief at not being alone anymore. "Oh, I know. I want to get to Mercy, too. Grandma Miller is all by herself at the ranch. She's got to be so worried about us! And she'll need our help. Dad and me, I mean. There's no way she can do all the work by herself."

Danny smiled at him, and gestured to the other two horses, one of them laden with supplies. "You're bringing a lot more to this arrangement than we are."

"Are you serious?" Ethan protested. "You have a flashlight! I'd give almost everything on that mare just to have it!"

Sam chuckled and patted Ethan on the back. "I'll explain how it works later. I'm sure we can find some more if we get creative about where we look. But we *do* need to decide what we're going to do about the whole horses versus bikes dilemma."

Ethan scratched at his head. Sam was right. There were three horses and three of them. If they left the bikes behind, but ran into his dad, then they'd be short a horse, and without any bikes. "We could always ride double if we needed to," he finally suggested.

"What about all of our gear?" Danny asked, while climbing down from Tango's back. "Maybe we could divide it up and stuff it in our backpacks and just wear them?"

Ethan scrunched up his nose. "Nah, we don't need to do that. We can figure out a way to tie some of it on to each horse. And I can ride the one bare back."

149

Sam mulled it over while Danny went and began to get the bags in question off of the pack horse. "I don't know," he said. "I think I'd like to at least keep my bike for a few more days, even if your dad doesn't show up here. I can keep up."

Ethan shrugged at Sam, not really caring either way. So long as he didn't have to keep riding one, the guy could peddle all the way to Mercy and it wouldn't be any skin off his back. Anyway, his dad *would* show up.

He helped lift down the last backpack before gathering up the lead ropes of the three horses. One good thing about the farming region was that there were plenty of small streams and irrigation ditches crisscrossing the land along that section of Interstate 15.

He walked the horses over to the largest cluster of trees that were close by, which were growing along a stream. It was a perfect spot to tie the animals up. While he busied himself with that chore, Sam began to unfold their two tents about thirty feet away. Danny picked another grouping of trees to construct a fire pit for cooking dinner later, and then spread out their sleeping bags in the shade.

Ethan studied the terrain as the two adults began to debate about where to put the tents. Danny wanted to keep them in the shade, while Sam opted to have them away from the fire.

It was Ethan's second time through the area in as many days and he'd be happy when he could leave it behind for good. They were surround by low, rolling hills dotted with farmland. To the south, two cement silos stood out on the horizon as the tallest structures for miles in any direction. To the east, a line of mountains rose, their tops green with trees and the promise of shade and cooler temperatures. Down in the flats, although cooler the past couple of days, it still had to be in the eighties, which was likely the main reason hardly anyone else was out wandering about.

There *were* other people, just not that many. Ethan experienced a mixture of dread and excitement each time another figure stumbled into view. It could either be his dad, or another Decker waiting to take everything from them.

A hand on his shoulder made him jump and Ethan turned to find Sam staring at him. "Let's get camp set up. And you don't need to worry so much. Decker is gone and we aren't going to leave you. I promise."

Ethan would have never guessed how much of an impact those words would have on him, and he fought against a sudden flood of tears. Although he still desperately wanted his dad, the deep void he'd been experiencing for five days slammed shut with a physical equivalent of a punch to the stomach. He took a shuddering breath and managed a brief nod before turning away to hide his raw emotions.

A cold nose touched his hand and Ethan knelt down to greet his other new friend, Grace. The golden retriever seemed to know when he needed the extra nudge, literally, and he smiled at the dog. She licked his cheeks and it was then that Ethan realized he'd been crying. "It's okay," he whispered to Grace, kissing her on the top of her head. "It's okay now."

CHAPTER 24

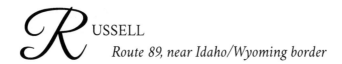

RUSSELL
Route 89, near Idaho/Wyoming border

RUSSELL MANEUVERED the mountain bike with a vigor he hadn't felt in some time. Though he somewhat regretted leaving the house behind, he moved forward with a sense of purpose. Things were lining up so perfectly that he was in awe of how he was orchestrating it all.

He steered around the burned-out shells of two wrecked cars, barely paying any notice to the remains lying over the steering wheel in the vehicle nearest him. Even on a less-used highway that connected a string of towns with populations of under five hundred, death and destruction were always present.

A fire burned in the distance to the west, likely having spread from a structure and into the woods. He'd passed a man and woman earlier in the day, on foot, who had told him to be careful of the fires raging to the north in and around Soda Springs,

Idaho. It was fire season to begin with, so everything was ripe for the burning.

Russell wasn't concerned. He was going to steer to the east of Idaho, and follow Highway 89 all the way north through Wyoming and straight into the Lewis and Clark National Park, where Mercy waited.

He grinned, thinking about his conversation with the young couple and how at ease they'd been with him. Russell looked down at his outfit, borrowed from the rich, globe-trotting home-owner. He wore loose-fitting athletic pants and a gray T-shirt with the words Live, Love, Laugh. When combined with his pleasant good looks, it made him quite approachable. He'd even given them some water. He wasn't a monster, after all.

"No, not a monster," Russell said to the empty road and trees that flew past. Something else. Something...*natural*. While he originally thought of the flashpoint as only the beginning of his own rebirth, he'd come to understand that it was much more than that. There was a comprehensive act of natural selection occurring; a purging, so to speak. The Earth had been building up to it for some time, and frankly, Russell was surprised the human species had continued for as long as it had. He didn't see himself as a prophet. Nothing that divine. Rather, he was an extension of the energy of the universe, a tool of nature. Only those worthy of surviving would be left when it was over. He had the ability to see that and the much, much larger picture of where they were headed.

Russell shifted his backpack and considered stopping for a short break. His shoulders were getting sore and it was close to dinner time. He still had a couple of hours before it got dark, although it didn't matter because he wasn't in any real rush. He wasn't on a schedule.

Coming to a stop in the gravel along the side of the road, Russell lowered his sunglasses and gazed out at the surrounding landscape. It was a winding section of road that worked its way through a series of low hills that he imagined led to more farmland. There wasn't anyone to be seen, which was how he preferred it.

Slipping the large trekking pack from his back, Russell realized how heavy it had become. He'd switched out the smaller backpack for it, after finding the larger bag in the garage of the lake house. Apparently, the owner's travels also included the kind that took them on vast hiking excursions. A duffle bag was attached to the back of his bike with a bungee cord, which was where he'd stuffed his small tent and a couple of other camping items. After five days on the road, he'd come up with a rather efficient way to travel and camp. Of course, he was a simple man to begin with and didn't like to complicate things. He only cared about meeting his basic needs.

Before Russell had a chance to take anything out, he heard an unusual noise. Freezing with his hand on the zipper of the bag, he tilted his head. Yes...there it was again. The whinny of a horse.

Russell took out some binoculars and then stepped away from the pack, letting it fall to the ground. In spite of the physical effort it took to travel by bike, he hadn't changed his mind about riding a horse. He had no desire to find one, but he was curious as to who was with the horses. He realized as he continued to listen that there was definitely more than one.

It was coming from farther up the road. Russell stepped off the highway and into the trees, quickly traversing the rugged terrain and cresting a small hill. He leaned against an outcropping of large rocks and raised the binoculars. Located about a hundred feet away was a group of eight horses. They'd had their saddles removed already and were tied to some trees by a small stream.

Near them, several men dressed in military garb were silently going about setting up a camp. One of them must have said something amusing, because another man laughed and then they continued erecting a canvas tent.

Russell could have felt threatened, and maybe an ordinary man would have. Instead he was intrigued. It was the first sign of any organized government activity. That they were riding horses instead of Humvees spoke volumes on its own, but he wanted...*needed* to know more.

Slipping away from the vantage point, Russell calmly returned to his gear and took out the deputy's shirt he'd packed away. He'd have to make do with his blue jeans to accompany it, since Mr. Rogers' pants hadn't been his size. He imagined the soldiers would respond better to a man in uniform.

After changing, he got back on the bike without eating and peddled up the road, whistling so that his arrival was announced in advance. No sense in testing the universe with a surprise encounter with men armed with automatic rifles.

As Russell rounded the curve, he acted shocked when he saw the group of soldiers off to the side of the road. Two of them had come out onto the highway with their rifles to intercept him. "Hello!" Russell called out, sounding relieved. "You can't imagine how happy I am to see you."

The two soldiers exchanged a look and kept their ARs slung across their chests, relaxed but at the ready. "Sorry to disappoint you, we're not here to render aid," the larger of the two men said. "We're on our way to an assignment at the reservoir."

Russell glanced behind them at what he hadn't been able to see from his lookout in the woods. They had two carts that the horses were pulling, likely full of whatever supplies they were transporting to the lake. They were in for a surprise when they got there, and it was all he could do not to laugh.

Instead, he gave a small nod of understanding and lifted his hands in a placating gesture. "I get it. Not to worry, I don't need anything. I'm doing better than most of the people I've seen south of here, though, so you might want to keep your heads on a swivel."

Another man walked out to join the conversation, and based on how the first two reacted, Russell assumed he was in command. "You local law enforcement? Where are you from?"

Russell stood straddling his bike, his backpack covering up part of his badge. Shifting his weight, he pulled the shoulder strap aside and smiled confidently. "Yes, sir. Well, not local so much to here, more like south of here in Rich County. Near Randolph, to be more exact. Deputy Rogers." He held out a hand.

The commander hesitated for only a moment, and then closed the space between them. As he took Russell's hand in a firm grip, the other two soldiers stood down, relaxing their stance and letting the ARs hang from their straps. "Sergeant Klinger, US Army Reserves. I don't mean to be rude, Deputy, but I'll have to ask that you keep moving."

His smile widening as they shook hands, Russell leaned back and gave a curt shake of his head. "No offense. I get it. I do wonder if you could answer a couple of questions for me first?"

"It was a gamma-ray burst," Sergeant Klinger said without preamble. "Over a third of the world's population wiped out, and an EMP destroyed almost all of our electronics."

Russell frowned and did his best to look morose. "I'd heard that it was a gamma-ray, but I had no idea the destruction was so widespread."

"Gamma radiation is to blame for a lot of it," the sergeant explained. "You're likely experiencing a mild case of exposure. Headache? Nausea?"

Russell nodded.

"It affects everyone differently and from here west, it's pretty mild for most people except the very young, old, or those with previous illnesses." Sergeant Klinger gestured to Russell's bike.

"Decent mode of transportation, but have you considered a horse?"

Russell smiled again. "I've never had much luck with them, and I don't mind the exercise. Can you tell me what it is you're doing at the reservoir?" he asked, getting to what he really wanted to know. "You're the first sign of any organized military I've seen and I'd like to know what the state of the government is. My own county was basically destroyed by fire and what wasn't burned got looted. The lawlessness was so bad that I decided to travel north, to my hometown in Montana."

Sergeant Klinger shook his head. "There is no civilian government. Martial law has been declared and General Montgomery is calling the shots out of Cheyenne Mountain in Colorado. We're establishing camp—I mean, FEMA shelters in the most populated locations, though our ranks are still pretty loose. After a week, we've just gotten to where we've established communication at the state and county level, and have begun reporting back to Cheyenne. The reservoir is a vital resource for supplying water to the shelters in Idaho and Utah." The sergeant pointed at the carts. "We're the first in our state to get an official assignment, but we're slowly getting there. As you already pointed out, we first have to establish some sort of control."

"Give it another week without aid, and there won't be nearly as many left to control," Russell stated, his voice a little more even keeled than he'd intended.

Sergeant Klinger cocked his head and squinted at Russell. "Our goal is to find a way to do both," he said.

"That's very ambitious." Russell knew he'd overstayed his welcome, but he also knew there was a purpose to meeting these men. The government was rounding up survivors into camps. How very convenient. "Anything I need to know in regard to the martial law? New rules I should be following?"

Sergeant Klinger took a couple of measured steps to the side, allowing room for Russell to pass. "Keep to yourself and you shouldn't have any issues. We'll be requisitioning needed supplies and structures to ensure the people's survival."

It was clearly a scripted response, and very telling. They weren't going to stop at the camps, or shelters, as they were calling them. It seemed the whole country, or what was left of it, was being treated as a militarized zone. It made sense. In order to save as many people as possible, the military would have to round them up and protect them from destroying each other and what was left. Russell smiled. He could work with that.

Instead of peddling away, he leaned forward and did his best imitation of a small-town cop rubbing elbows with another lawman. "Let me tell you about my hometown."

CHAPTER 25

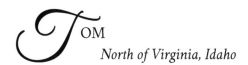

OM

North of Virginia, Idaho

"I WON'T STOP until I find my son." Tom whispered the words in the gathering darkness, like an oath or mantra. One he'd used to keep himself going for the past two days. He was still groggy at times and although he'd intended to ride through the previous night nonstop so he'd arrive in Virginia by that afternoon, his body had other plans. He'd fallen asleep in the saddle. Or passed out, it didn't really matter which.

He'd been lucky. The sun on his face woke him up that morning and Tom found himself lying slumped on the horse's neck. They had stopped at a creek near the freeway, not far from where he last remembered riding. Fortunately, no one had come by and decided to help themselves to his things while he'd been out, and he'd pushed on.

Tom looked out at the darkening expanse of fields and considered his options. He was now only a few miles north of the small town where he hoped to find Ethan. After taking a wide path around Pocatello, he'd been unable to pick up their trail on the other side. No matter how hard he searched the hardpacked earth to either side of the freeway, or how many people he questioned, he didn't come up with any positive results. There were simply too many survivors wandering the road near the city, and more people were traveling by horse.

His head was clearer than it had been in days, and he knew that his best chance of locating Ethan was in Virginia, but it wasn't going to happen in the dark. There was a chance he could pass right by them and not even realize it.

Slowing his horse, Tom took a couple of deep breaths to center himself. That's when he noticed how cold it was getting. In actuality, it was probably still in the low fifties, but in comparison to the heat he'd been suffering through it was a sharp contrast. Shivering, he dismounted and wished he had his sweatshirt. He'd been wearing the same outfit now for a week, and he both smelled and looked like it.

Rubbing a hand across his stubbly chin, he led the horses to the only tree near them. The same network of streams and irrigation canals they'd been by all day were close by and he'd let the animals have their fill once he'd gotten something to eat. He hadn't had any food since that morning and he paused, confused.

Had he eaten?

Shaking his head to clear the haze that threatened to settle in again, he admitted to himself that he wasn't okay. He understood his situation and that he was still suffering from a concussion, but there wasn't anything he could do about it at the moment.

The cut over his eye was festering, and though he'd washed the blood from his face, it was still swollen and covered in bruises. At least his shoulder was healing well. Tom rotated it, stretching the muscles and testing the level of pain the movement caused. Grunting in satisfaction, he remembered again that he still needed to eat. That was the main symptom of the concussion. He was constantly getting distracted and forgetting what he was doing, or finding himself simply staring out into space, unsure of where or who he was for a fleeting moment.

"Food," Tom said to Lilly, who nickered at him softly in response. She was a good horse. Her full name was Lilly Of The Valley, he assumed because she was a solid white. The other brown mare wasn't quite as personable, but they were both strong and he'd be forever grateful to Ed and Marnie.

The horses reminded Tom of home and he closed his eyes for a moment, wishing the random thought would go away. He knew how worried his mom was and how hard it must be for her, all alone on the ranch. He distracted himself from thinking about his friends and family by lifting down his bag and rummaging in it for something he didn't have to cook.

He'd need to find some more food soon. Ed had shoved some non-perishables into his backpack, but the crackers and jerky were almost gone. Opting for a Pop-Tart and small bag of Doritos, Tom absently shoved chips into his mouth while he studied the ground. It was dark enough that it was hard to see, though it looked as good a place as any to spread out his sleeping bag. He briefly debated setting up the tent Ed gave him, finding the task felt overwhelming even though he was cold.

"Come on," he said to Lilly as he picked up her lead rope. Popping half of the Pop-Tart into his mouth, he walked out into the field in search of the water that was out there somewhere. He already regretted not stopping sooner, when it was still light out. Why wasn't he being smarter about things?

Tom was injured, and was pushing himself too hard. Physically, mentally, he was breaking down, yet it didn't matter. Nothing mattered except Ethan.

"I won't stop until I find my son," he said slowly and with a tight control of his emotions. He had to stay focused.

A flicker of orange light in the distance made him stop. He stood staring at it for a full minute before deciding that it was, in fact, a fire. A campfire.

His adrenaline spiking, Tom was impatient with the horses and finally tied them up near the water, rather than going back to where he'd left his things. He'd get them later.

The odds of the people sitting around the fire being Ethan and his abductors were incredibly small, but Tom had to know. He'd simply sneak up and confirm it wasn't Ethan, before going back and getting some much-needed sleep. He'd get to Virginia in the morning and start asking around. It was a tiny hole in the wall, and the three of them with their horses would stand out.

Tom moved with a grace that was unusual in a man of his size, and it allowed him to get close without being heard or seen. Some distance from the fire, he heard the horses before he saw them. His breath coming faster, Tom saw a light bobbing, headed toward him.

"What the—" Tom breathed when he realized it was a *flash-light* he was seeing. Blinking a couple of times, he ignored the implications and instead focused on who was holding it. They were in total darkness now, and with the light out in front of him, it was impossible for Tom to make out the other man's features.

He eased closer to the trees and horses, the tall, dew-laden grass masking his movement. The horse nearest him whinnied and tossed its head, catching a corner of the beam of light. It was Tango.

Tom's nostrils flared. It was Ethan's horse and the only other thing he was certain of was that the man moving closer was *not* his son. He was too big, his shoulders too broad. Kneeling down, Tom felt blindly around on the ground until his hand closed over a large stick. He chastised himself for not taking the time at some point during his trek to find something he could use as a weapon.

Now, he'd have to make do with what he could find, even if it meant going up against armed men with a tree branch. It never occurred to him to leave and form a plan. He was single-minded in his desperation and not thinking clearly.

As the man walked past Tom on his way to Tango, he stood and without any hesitation, brought the stick down like a club with all of his strength. It connected with the back of the man's head with a sickening thud and he staggered forward three steps before dropping, the flashlight disappearing into the thick grass.

Tom didn't even stop to check and see if he was unconscious, he was already moving toward the fire when the other man hit the ground. Tom's heart hammered in his ears, and his vision was narrowed. Time felt as if it were slowing down and he was moving through a heavy atmosphere.

Tom saw the fire, about thirty feet away. As he neared, two figures came into view, one with their back to him. On the other side of the campfire a smaller shape huddled under a sleeping bag, his head drooping.

Tom's breath caught. It was Ethan. His son, wrapped in a sleeping bag, his face so battered that he hardly recognized him. Fury welled up in Tom's chest, a hatred so strong that it scared him. He would kill whoever had done that to his son. With his bare hands, he'd kill him.

Tom shifted his attention to the target of his vengeance. The man's back was to him, and he was also wrapped in a sleeping bag, but he wasn't asleep. He was moving, turning towards him, likely having heard Tom as he'd begun running.

All Tom could think of in that moment was that he couldn't get shot. He was taken back to the day on the trail, when he'd let his guard down and had failed at protecting his son. It would never happen again.

A guttural cry of rage escaped Tom as he threw himself into the other man's back and knocked him to the ground.

CHAPTER 26

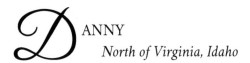ANNY
North of Virginia, Idaho

DANNY GAZED up at the night sky, thinking that she'd never get used to the constant presence of the northern lights. They were extremely bright that night, with dark purple pillars cutting through the bluish-white billowing ribbons. She missed seeing the stars.

She opened her mouth to make a comment about it to Ethan, when she noticed that the boy had fallen asleep. Grinning, she leaned out and tossed another stick on the small fire they had going. It was the first time in several days that they'd kept one burning after eating dinner. The first few nights, the light had brought a peace of mind, but lately, it just made it too hot to sleep. Not that night, though.

Danny sat back on the log and pulled her sleeping bag back up, all the way to her head. She couldn't get warm, which was a strange sensation to have after melting in the heat for a week.

She looked back up at the lights and frowned. What were the odds that the atmosphere was extra-weird the same night that it was unseasonably cool? The storm with the odd lightning from the other night still weighed on her mind. Things were off, and in a world where everything else was turned inside-out, she'd hoped to at least be able to count on Mother Nature to keep it together.

Shaking her head, Danny wondered what was keeping Sam. He worried too much about the horses and had already checked on them twice now since they'd stopped. But that was just Sam being Sam, and she knew better than to try and control him. Danny had learned that much, at least, during their time together.

Grace snored from where she was curled up at Ethan's feet under the sleeping bag with him. The two were inseparable, and Danny was trying not to be jealous. She didn't blame Grace; the kid was pretty likable and in obvious need of a friend. The golden retriever was a perfect candidate since all she did was offer companionship without asking any questions.

Danny prayed they'd find Ethan's dad, but chances were that it would be back at the rest stop where he'd last seen him. She wasn't sure how they'd handle that, when the time came. The only thing she *was* sure of was that she'd be delivering Ethan home to his grandma at the Miller Ranch, no matter what. Ethan told them all about it, describing the rolling pastures and private lakes all backed up to the rugged mountains surrounding the valley. Danny was looking forward to visiting, after she had a nice, long reunion with her dad.

Her brows drew together at the thought of her own father. While Ethan seemed confident in his grandma's ability to fend for herself, it was different for her dad. Maybe she was underestimating him. Rubbing her hands together under the sleeping bag, Danny tried to talk herself down from the building anxiety. The beta-blockers he took slowed his heart rate and lowered his blood pressure. He had narrowing of his coronary arteries, which was what led to his heart attack. If his pressure got too high and his heart rate went unchecked, it was only a matter of time before he suffered another, more serious heart attack, or else a stroke.

A sound behind her broke through her thoughts, and Danny started to turn, ready to give Sam a hard time for spending so much time obsessing over the horses. She registered something wasn't right before she'd completed the turn. The steps were too heavy and coming too fast. Sam wouldn't be running...*rushing* at her.

Before Danny had a chance to react, someone big slammed into her back, knocking her off the log, and the breath from her lungs. Stunned, she reacted without thinking, rolling onto her back and shoving at her attacker, attempting to push him off her. The face she looked into was so unexpected that she stopped struggling for a heartbeat to grasp what she was seeing.

The man's shaggy black hair blended with his beard to obscure part of his features, but his intense green eyes were terrifying. They were wild with a savage bloodlust she'd never seen before. His face was swollen in places and shaded with healing bruises. His teeth flashed white in the dim light as he snarled and it compelled her to move.

Bringing her legs up she planted her feet solidly against the man's chest and kicked out with all of her strength. Just before she launched him several feet through the air, his expression changed. His brows came together and his mouth opened in surprise, perhaps recognizing for the first time that his opponent was a woman.

Danny didn't care. She wouldn't let anyone ever hurt the boy again, and it certainly wasn't going to be by some crazed lunatic. Scrambling to her feet, she reached for the 1911 that was secured in the leg holster she'd made earlier in the day. As she drew it, she became aware of Grace barking and Ethan shouting. Unable to decipher what he was saying, she held up her other hand, motioning for him to stay back.

"Stop!" Ethan screamed when the gun came out, struggling to untangle himself from the sleeping bag. "Stop, Danny!"

Danny squared off with the large man as she raised the gun. He'd already gotten to his feet and was gasping for air, also holding a cautionary hand out to Ethan. His eyes flitted from Ethan, to the growling dog, and then to the weapon. Instead of the fear Danny expected to see, it was more like…recognition.

The only reason she hadn't already pulled the trigger was because it was the last bullet and she didn't want to miss. By the time she'd lined up the shot, Danny realized that something was off. Aside from being attacked by a wild man, none of it made sense, and there was something familiar about him. The way he stood, the shape of his jaw, the color of his eyes.

"Dad!" Ethan was crying now and moved in between the gun and the man, blocking the shot Danny had already decided not to take.

Tom threw his arms around his son, obviously confused and looking at Danny over Ethan's head like she was still an adversary.

Sam staggered into the firelight then, moaning and holding a hand to the back of his head. He took one look at Tom and Ethan and then cautiously approached Danny. Reaching out, he placed a hand over hers, pushing it down. She'd still been pointing the gun at them, and holding her breath. Danny made a small whimpering sound as she drew a ragged breath and fought against the fight-or-flight response surging through her body.

"It's okay," Sam urged, taking the weapon from her.

Her heart still racing, Danny managed to blink a few times and took a step back. Grace came to her and she knelt down, reaching out blindly for the dog. Tasting blood, Danny dabbed at the corner of her mouth, then gingerly touched her right cheek, where her face had taken the brunt of the fall. It was going to leave a mark. The man sure had a way of making an entrance.

Ethan stepped back then and looked over at Sam and Danny, the bruises unable to mask his happiness. "It's okay, you guys," he said, his smile growing. He turned back to Tom and hugged him again, his voice muffled as he spoke against his broad chest.

"This is my dad."

Made in the USA
Lexington, KY
04 December 2019